My Daddy's Baby

A Novel

by
Charmaine Marie

My Daddy's Baby

Published By: Real L.O.V.E. Publications

www.projectreallove.org

Cover Design By:

Chanel Smith

WPD Media

Cover Photograph:

Tyeisha Tucker

My Daddy's Baby

This novel is a work of fiction. Names, descriptions, entities, and incidents included in the story are exclusively products of the author's imagination. Any resemblance to actual persons, events, and entities is entirely coincidental.

ISBN#: 9781734255102

Printed in the United States of America

My Daddy's Baby

At an early age our grandparents instilled the principles of God, the seeds of love, and the value of family. You extend that same love and value throughout your community. We have watched you grow into a woman of undeniable faith, perseverance, and determination. We are honored to celebrate with you in your many life accomplishments. It is with much respect and admiration that we congratulate you, our cousin, Charmaine Marie, on your book, My Daddy's Baby.

With Much Love,

LaShonda Badgett
On behalf of: The Cousins
The Hodges Family

DEDICATION

I dedicate this book to my wonderful mother, Millie Lemon. Thank you for always speaking positivity into my life and encouraging and motivating me. Thank you for supporting me, pushing me to be my best at all times, instilling in me that the sky is the limit, and for giving me the truth when I choose anything other than greatness.

I love you Mom!

———

To my wife, Millie Lemon, from your husband and best friend, Thomas Lemon Sr. My wife is a retired counselor. I love, adore, and respect her. She cares deeply about people and youth are her passion.

Loving unconditionally is what she does

and greatness is what she stands for.

I love you Mil!

———

To my mother, Millie Lemon, from your daughter, Elaine Tucker. Mom, I love you. When I was younger, I don't think I realized your value. Thank you for being here for me over and over again, regardless of how I acted or treated you. Thank you for supporting me throughout my journey of womanhood. Thank you for always reminding me about the big picture. Thank you most of all for being my mom.

You were my mom first and I love you.

I know you always say there's no book to teach motherhood,

you are very correct, but you did an amazing job.

I love you Mom!

———

My Daddy's Baby

To my sister, from your sister Evie Hodges-Greene, on behalf of your siblings. My sister Millie is a very loving, thoughtful, and caring person. She's always anxious to help me whenever I need her. Thank you, Millie. She's a self-starter and a very motivated educator. My sister is a wonderful mother, grandmother, and great grandmother.

Yes, I said great grandmother.

We love you Millie!

———

To my aunt, from your niece Brittany Hodges, on behalf of all the cousins. For generations, Aunt Mildred "Millie" Hodges-Lemon, has continued to inspire those around her. As a beloved sister, mother, grandmother, aunt, educator and more, Aunt Millie champions for others to be the best version of themselves and does so with conviction! It's evident she is no stranger to hard work and this resonates with us all when she shares the many obstacles and triumphs she's faced during her lifetime; because sometimes rather than wait for a door to open, you need to simply build your own door! She is kind, humble, loving, witty, and a vital piece to the puzzle of our family and we are proud to call her "Aunt Millie". (She can also tell you all of the good restaurants within a 50mile radius)

We love you!

———

My Daddy's Baby

To Grandma Millie, from your grandson, Tierre Maclin, on behalf of
all the grandchildren and great-grandchildren. I'm not sure exactly
where to begin, but I appreciate your wisdom and "relatability".
Your resistance to a status quo existence
has inspired me to keep pressing forward.
I appreciate your support and advice over the years,
and I'm thankful that you've been an example of the hard work
I should put behind my faith in a more positive future
for myself, and the community.
Thanks for being here for us.
We love you!

———

To Millie Lemon, from your former student, mentee, and friend,
Tabitha Demarest. To my mentor from high school to this present day:
like Naomi stuck with Ruth, you persevered with me. Thank you for
teaching me how to always land on my feet! I love you dearly! Special
thanks to Laini and Charmaine for unselfishly sharing your precious
mother with me, the community, and the world!
I love you!

———

1

With a membership of five thousand, Intentional Deliverance
Nondenominational Church was packed with people this fine Sunday
morning, and their spirits were very, very high. Eight people were going
to be baptized today. This was not unusual in this house of God; they
were always winning souls to Christ.

"We baptize you in the name of Jesus, and you shall receive the
precious gift of the Holy Ghost," the Associate Pastor, First Lady Alma
Ruth Hodges, said as she baptized Jermaine Riley III. He was ready
and willing. You could tell the Holy Ghost, being the gentleman, he is,
was about to move something.

This man was blessing the Lord like never before. You could clearly
hear the "Hallelujah" and the "Thank You, Jesus" as he jumped up and
down with his fists tightly pointing up, his body slightly bent over, and
his head facing down. This was an exciting moment for the church. The
glory of the Lord was raining down in this place. And there it was—the
new tongue he was looking for, his direct connection with God the
Father. The Holy Ghost took over his lips as he cried out in a language,
only he and God could understand. Out of his belly, rivers of living water
flowed.

Raquel could not believe it, her father, of all people had decided to go
down in Jesus name. What a change for the better. She thought that this
day in her life and in her father's life, would never come. She knew

today, better than any other day, that there really is a God in heaven who can turn the heart of the wicked.

Jermaine Marquice Riley III was a handsome, six-foot-two tall man with a bald head and a thin goatee. His gray pin-striped Steve Harvey suit fit him really good that morning and it made no sense how good he smelled. He caught every single woman's eyes and even the married women had to turn their heads as he walked by. Jermaine had a diamond earring in his left ear that blinged like crazy against the church lights. He always wore his platinum chain, with a platinum diamond cross hanging on it, to church. His platinum watch with diamonds around the face was top of the line too.

Jermaine had been attending church faithfully now for the last three months. It had been a tremendous, lifechanging event for him that could not have come at a better time. The original reason he came to church service, was to follow up behind his new woman friend, Shela Renee Johnston. Not particularly interested in hearing the word of God, he just wanted to make a good impression on Evangelist Shela.

As always, God had alternative plans for Jermaine. It was not long before the word of God took over his mind and soul, and he was beating her to the church, fervently wanting to learn more about her Lord.

Jermaine knew the church had changed his life and that the saints of God had his best interest at heart. He also knew that this was the place he wanted to call home. He had invited his only daughter, Raquel Riley, that morning because he was going to get baptized. He wanted her to be there for that special moment, and he wanted her to join too.

"Raquel, I'm going to go up and join this morning, and I want you to go with me."

"What? Wow, Dad! I think that's great, but do I have to go with you? I've never been here before," she whispered.

"Yes, you do. I want us to go up there together, and from now on, you are going to be coming with me and Shela every Sunday morning."

"Okay, Dad. I guess I have no choice. It's all good." She sat there with her lips poked out, however, after a while Raquel started grinning and thinking very deeply. She was very happy her dad found the Lord, and she knew this was a big step for them.

"Do we have anyone who would like to join the church this morning?" Senior Pastor Oscar Joseph Hodges asked.

Jermaine and Raquel stood up, held hands, and walked down the aisle to join. This Sunday, there were five other people who joined: a husband, his wife, and their two-month-old daughter, an older woman with a big blue hat that had diamonds around it with a white bow, and a young man who looked to be about eighteen years old. You could tell the church was happy as they gave the new members the right hand of fellowship.

Immediately after service was dismissed, the First Lady came over to invite Shela and her friends over for dinner. Shela was one of Lady Hodges's armor-bearers. She was very excited and proud to have been invited over for dinner, because this would be the first time she did not go alone. She was even more excited to have the finest man in the church and his beautiful daughter going with her. Excitedly, they all accepted the offer. Soon after that, they walked outside to get in Shela's fully loaded custom-made four-door 2019 Bentley Continental GT convertible.

Raquel loved riding in Shela's car. It was the most beautiful car she had ever seen, and her hair could blow in the wind. Shela spoiled Raquel more than her father did, and Raquel just loved it. She gave her anything she wanted, everything was always done her way, and her opinion was asked about everything they did.

As they pulled up to a gated community with mansions inside, Raquel's mouth opened wide. She was excited and speechless all at the same time. Shela reached over to put the gate code in, and Raquel started shaking her head from side to side in disbelief.

"Wow, so this is where the pastor lives?" Raquel said. "I can't believe it. I guess my friends are right, God is good because this don't make no sense!"

They pulled up at 10933 Scott Street, where stood the largest, most beautiful home on the block, surrounded by a black iron fence. The immaculate manor with a four-car garage had landscape resembling a tropical paradise. Shela slowly pulled up the driveway where there were two other luxury cars already parked.

As they all got out of the car, Raquel looked around in total amazement. You could clearly tell she had never been in a neighborhood like this before. She and her best friends, Delila and Martine, had always believed that Martine's house was a mansion, but boy were they wrong! As they got up to the door, they were greeted by Noelle, the family's teacup pup, jumping up and down in the glass window. She was so pretty in her tiny pink sweater that read "Noelle" and her pink ribbons that were neatly placed on both of her ears.

"Greetings," First Lady Hodges said as she opened the door and hugged everyone as they came in. "How are you doing?"

With smiles on their faces, they all answered that they were well.

"This is the most beautiful house I have ever seen," Raquel said. "May I have a tour?"

"Raquel! Stop it!" Jermaine said with much authority, looking her in the eyes with embarrassment. "They don't feel like doing all that."

"No, it's okay," First Lady Hodges said. "I don't mind at all. Come on, Raquel."

"Thank you so much," Raquel said eagerly. She smiled at her father in amusement and walked away, laughing at him.

This two-story house was breathtaking. It had marble floors with underfloor heating, a European-design spiral staircase, three fireplaces, a finished basement, eight bathrooms, and seven bedrooms. Pastor Hodges had designed and built this house. He was in the architecture business for over forty years. He passed down his company, A & O Hodges Architect Systems, to his sons, Oscar Hodges Jr. and Marzee Hodges. This was the most successful architect business in Omaha, Nebraska, and they planned on carrying out this legacy forever.

Lady Hodges had really put her foot in the meal today. She prepared stuffed peppers with ground beef, cheese, onions, green beans, white rice, freshly baked from scratch crescent rolls, cherry limeade to drink, and pineapple upside-down cake for dessert. They were having dinner in the formal dining area that seated ten people and using fine china, only used for special occasions.

"Everyone bow your heads please," Pastor Hodges said, "So I can pray over the food. Father, in the name of Jesus, we ask that you would bless this food and that it would provide nourishment to our body. We pray that you would bless the hands that prepared the food, and we thank you for providing us with this food. Lord, we thank you for all these things in the precious name of Jesus. Amen."

"Amen," everyone replied.

Everyone ate and enjoyed the great cooking. They talked and laughed and got more acquainted with one another. Suddenly, Pastor Hodges started asking questions about his spiritual daughter, Shela.

"What are your intentions, Son?"

"My intentions?" Jermaine said with a confused look on his face.

"Yes, Son, your intentions with Shela! I have been seeing you around for a few months now. Surely you have some kind of intentions."

Without hesitations, Jermaine proudly said, "Well, yes, Sir, I believe she is the woman God has always wanted me to have in my life. She is perfect, and I want to share the rest of my life with her."

The news shocked the whole table. Everyone looked around at each other widemouthed, especially Shela.

"So, Shela, what about you? You have been hanging out with Jermaine quite a bit lately. I have never seen this type of behavior with you. What do you think of Jermaine? It appears he has great interest in you. How do you feel?"

"Well, Dad," Shela replied. "The last three months of my life, have been the best three months of my life. Honestly, I have never met a man so great. I, too, believe he was sent straight from God."

"Bless the Lord, oh my soul," Lady Hodges said. "This is so exciting. I hear wedding bells. Does anyone else hear what I hear? Raquel, Sweetie, what do you think?"

"I am so happy for my dad and Shela. Shela is the best thing that has happened to us since my mother passed away. She has changed the whole atmosphere of our home. I love her, and I hope and pray she stays around forever. My dad could not have found a better woman."

"I am sorry to hear about your mother passing, but I am so happy you are happy with Shela," Lady Hodges said.

"Thanks a lot, but it's okay about my mom and all. I can't say I don't miss her, and she could never be replaced, but Shela is just what I needed, and she came right on time. The more my day goes by, the more I keep getting confirmation about what my friends have been trying to tell me forever—that God is truly good. Wow!"

"Jermaine, what areas are you interested in serving at the church?" Pastor Hodges asked.

"Serving?" Jermaine cleared his throat. "Well, Pastor, I had not given it much thought at all. I have so many things going on in my life. All I really need right now is the word of God. I had planned on just coming to church and continuing to worship and praise the Lord."

"Son, you know I would love for you to come on board with my armor-bearers. You seem like you would be a great protector of your pastor. What do you think?"

"I mean, I don't have anything against it, but what exactly would I have to do?" Jermaine chuckled a little, as he noticed that Pastor Hodges had totally ignored what he had just said about just coming to church.

"First of all, you must be a member of the church. You need to be saved, sanctified, and filled with the Holy Ghost. You need to be a faithful tither, and you will have to get on the schedule and be willing to protect your pastor. My armor-bearers can explain the rest of it to you, if you are interested."

"I don't have a problem with any of that," Jermaine said. "I probably need to be active in the church doing something anyway, I guess. I don't have an issue with any of those requirements, and yes, I am all of the above. Shela is serious about the tithing thing, and she made sure I understand it and do it. That is one of her requirements."

Suddenly, Raquel started feeling very nauseated and asked to be excused from the table so she could use the bathroom. When she got in the bathroom, she could feel her stomach turning, and she immediately leaned over the toilet and threw up everything she had just eaten.

This was very abnormal for Raquel as she never got sick. Although her food was good, she figured something had to be wrong with it. Obviously, First Lady's food was old or spoiled or something.

2

Shela Renee Johnston was the reason why Jermaine Riley III was at Intentional Deliverance Nondenominational Church. They had become friends about four months ago and began dating immediately. Shela was an evangelist and held that position for ten years. She was a true servant of the Lord, and was on just about every auxiliary at her church. Shela was a very pretty, short, dark-skinned, solid, classy woman who always dressed to impress and had the most gracious and friendly attitude. There's no one she could not get along with because she was just so loveable. Shela had no children, but always desired having them. At forty-three years old now, her prayer was to get married and have children soon.

Shela lived out in Regency on the west side of Omaha, Nebraska, with a beautiful house having four bedrooms, three-and-a-half baths, a two-car garage, a movie room, and a "Diva Den". She bought the land and built the house five years previously and paid cash for it. There were vaulted ceilings and accent walls, along with a big beautiful fireplace in her living room and tile flooring throughout the house.

Shela was the head prosecutor in Douglas County. She worked at the courthouse since she was seventeen years old. She started out as a Customer Service Representative and worked her way up to the top. She'd always been an honor roll student, and since she was an outstanding employee for at least a year, the county paid for her to go to college. At twenty-one, she graduated at the top of her class from

Creighton University, where she received her Bachelor of Arts Degree in Legal Studies. Then she went on to receive her Master of Arts Degree in Law from the same college. Since she had no children and almost no responsibilities, she was able to go and receive her Juris Doctorate, Degree in Law, by the time she turned twenty-nine years old.

Shela was "Top Dawg" in the state of Nebraska, and well known in all the surrounding cities. She did not play when it came to criminal justice. She was a no-nonsense woman, and everyone knew it. Shela was particularly hard on sex offenders. That was just what she was known for. No one had ever questioned why, but just because of the fact that they might have to face her as a prosecutor, the sex offender rate dropped drastically in the state of Nebraska. She requested maximum punishment every time someone was found guilty, because she believed it was a senseless and unforgiveable crime.

Shela had always believed in abstaining from sexual activity until she was married—until she met Jermaine Riley III, that is. She had never met a guy that fine who was so well put together. He appeared to be the best father to his only daughter, Raquel Riley, and he gave her everything she wanted and needed. He worked as Lead Customer Service Representative at Telemarketing Professionals, and had been there for the last ten years. Jermaine had wined and dined Shela since the day he met her. No one had ever treated her so well. He opened all her doors, carried all her bags, and took her anywhere she wanted to go. She never had to worry about the tab or the tip.

Shela knew she had found the man of her dreams, and that the man of her dreams had found a woman who was definitely wife material.

Since the second week of knowing Jermaine, she had cooked dinner for him and Raquel almost every night. She truly believed in catering to her man, something she had seen her mother do to her husband for the last thirty-six years. Not only did she cook dinner for Jermaine every night, but sometimes she made him breakfast in the morning. On those days, he usually stopped by on his way to work to get that.

The most Shela had ever willingly done with a man was kiss him, and she had not done that in ten years. She'd had plenty of boyfriends, but none was ever worth compromising her values and standards. She was able to get her status in life by leaving men out of the equation, however, Jermaine was different. He was the man she had been waiting on all her life.

3

Jermaine was the perfect gentleman. He always greeted Shela with a hug, a kiss, and a gift. It was three months ago when Jermaine spent the night for the first time at her house. He was sleeping in one of the spare bedrooms, and Raquel was sleeping in the room she calls hers while Shela slept in her room. In the middle of the night, Jermaine could no longer sleep in that bed alone with a beautiful woman waiting in the next room, so he decided to go and love his woman.

As Jermaine opened the door, he heard Shela's light snoring, just like a baby, sleeping gracefully and peacefully. He stood over her, smiling, rubbing his goatee, and thinking of what he was going to do to please his woman. He lifted the blanket and climbed under it next to his fine woman. He pulled her toward him, and she opened her eyes and rolled over to put her arms around her handsome man. Jermaine proceeded to kiss his woman all over her body, which put her in a world she had heard about, but had never experienced. It was like paradise to the fourth power. She was inexperienced in this area but willing to learn, and her teacher had no problem explaining the art.

The next morning when Shela woke up, she was in total disbelief. What had seemed like a dream was a great reality that she did not regret taking place. The only question she had was, "Did we use a condom?" And of course, they did not. In a way,

Shela was hoping she was pregnant by this sexy man because her biological clock was ticking like crazy and there was no better time than the present. However, she thought about her position in the church and what the church folks would say. Then she thought about her loyalty to God, but she knew He would be the only one to truly forgive her.

Shela got up to cook breakfast, but her man met her downstairs and they cooked breakfast together. This turned her on even more. She loved the fact that he liked to do everything together. "What a man." She thought.

As Jermaine and Shela were hugging and kissing, Raquel walked in with a big smile on her face. Seeing her father happy again had been her desire for a long time, and Shela brought out the best in him.

"Look at you two love birds," Raquel said, going over to hug them both. "I just love it. When are you going to marry her Dad? What are you waiting for?"

Jermaine and Shela looked at Raquel with smiles on their faces.

"Soon, Honey, very soon."

"Wow, I can't wait," Shela said. "I love my man. I've got the best man walking. Thank you, Jesus."

"Yeah, I think you both lucked up this time," Raquel said with one hand on her hip and her finger pointing from Shela to Jermaine. "God blessed two great people with each other. It must be nice, guys."

"I can't complain," Jermaine said, shrugging his shoulders, and blowing Shela a kiss.

"Me either," Shela said, catching the kiss.

"You have nothing to complain about guys," Raquel said, as she went on looking into the pots and pans. "I'm hungry, and it smells good."

"Honey, I've got scrambled eggs, hash browns, sausage, bacon, homemade biscuits, grits, and orange juice," Jermaine said.

"That's a lot of food, huh, Raquel," Shela said, rubbing her stomach and feeling very excited.

"Yes, it is," Raquel said, with a big smile on her face.

"Go get washed up," Shela said, waving Raquel off toward the bathroom.

"I just washed my hands before I came down."

"Did you brush your teeth, Girl?"

They all laughed, took their seats at the kitchen table, and enjoyed their wonderful breakfast, as they talked about what they were going to do for the day.

4

Shela's parents met Jermaine and Raquel about three months ago. They thought he was a very nice guy and approved of him for their daughter. This was odd for Shela's father because he never thought anyone was good enough for his daughter. Shela's mother, Charai Christine Johnston, was a retired counselor; and her father, Jon DeWayne Johnston, a retired principal. Jon and Charai met when Shela was five years old and married when she was seven years old. When they got married, Jon adopted Shela. She never got to know her biological father, Shelton Rendel Dortch, because he was diagnosed with lung cancer at twenty-five years old and died before she was born.

Shela and her mother were best friends, and most of the time, Shela shared all her personal business with her. Shela called her mother so she could explain what had gone on with her and Jermaine about three months ago or so. Her mother was totally shocked because as far as she knew, Shela was saving herself for her husband, and had always been serious about abstaining from sexual activity, until she was married.

"So, Baby, you had sex with Jermaine, and you did not use any protection?" Mrs. Johnston said.

"Yes, Mom, I did. And, Mom, it was definitely an experience."

"Well, Baby, you know that Raquel is our grandchild, but it will be wonderful if you have a baby. Your father and I have been wanting you to get married and have a baby for years, so Shela, honestly, I am delighted and so happy for you. I think you could have waited until you got married, but that is neither here nor there. However, I am going to let you tell your father."

"Thanks, Mom. I am happy too, but remember, I am just saying I had sex. It's just that I have never felt the way I am feeling now, so I do not know if I am pregnant or not. But as soon as I know and my man knows, you will know."

5

"Pastor, your appointment, Jermaine Riley, is here," Aubrey Allbright said, as she called into Pastor Hodges's office.

"Alright, Aubrey, send him in please."

"Yes, Sir." Aubrey got up to escort Jermaine into Pastor Hodges's office.

"Good evening, Pastor."

"Good evening, Jermaine. How are you doing?"

"I am well, Pastor. And you?"

"I am blessed, Son."

"Great, Pastor. This is a beautiful office," Jermaine said as he looked all around. "I love it. I pray to have an office like this one day. This is exactly what I would expect a man of your stature to have. Any pastor who is as dedicated and true to their flock as you, deserves nothing but the best."

"I appreciate that, Son. I hear so many things, but it's the positive things that impact my way of thinking. Thanks a lot."

"You are very welcome, Sir."

"Jermaine, I am sure you are wondering why I called you into a meeting with me."

"Well, sort of."

"Okay, well, we talked about you being one of my armor-bearers. I would like to introduce you to my armor-bearers, and I want you to go to work immediately."

"Wow, Pastor! What an honor! Are you serious?"

"Yes, Son, I am. Do you have any problems with that?"

"No, Pastor, I don't have any problems with that, but—"

"But what, Son?" said Pastor Hodges.

"What about my past?"

"Son, your past does not define you."

"Okay," Jermaine said, shaking his head. He had a weird look on his face.

"Okay what, Son? You sound a little bit confused. You got saved, didn't you?"

"Yes, Sir."

"You accepted Jesus into your heart, right?"

"Yes, Sir."

"You have repented of all your sins, right?"

"Yes, Sir."

"So that alone says you have decided to make a change. You are a part of the new birth experience, right? You have been water baptized and received the precious gift of the Holy Ghost, right?"

"Yes, Sir."

"And now you are trying your best to live a saved, sanctified, righteous lifestyle, right?

"Yes, Sir."

"Well, Son, the Bible says, 'Old things are passed away and all things are made new.'"

"So, Pastor, what you are telling me is that from this point on, I need to move forward and not look back, because anything I've done in my past does not matter anymore?"

"Basically, Son, that's exactly what I am saying. Now the consequences of your past decisions, mistakes, and actions are still going to come. However, here at Intentional Deliverance Nondenominational Church, your past is your past, and don't let anyone haunt you with it."

"Okay, Pastor. I fully understand what you are saying, and I really appreciate you breaking that down for me. I really needed that."

"Son, you just keep coming to church to receive the word and allow it to penetrate your heart."

"Okay, Pastor."

"One more thing, Jermaine. I would also like to add you to our Deacon Board."

"Wow, Pastor, the Deacon Board? Those seasoned wise men, Pastor? Are you sure about that?"

"Son, I move as God moves me, and that is where I see you, Deacon Jermaine Riley III. What do you think?"

"Pastor, I'm taking it all in, and I am elated. I believe I can do it, and I think this is a true step for me into my destiny. Pastor, I accept the call." Jermaine stood up excitedly and went to hug Pastor Hodges. "Pastor, this is the first time in my life I have been accepted into an organization that has a worthy cause, and the first time in my life a real man has complimented me on anything. This is the first time in my life I am truly happy with myself. I thank you, Pastor, for everything you have done for me. Thanks for accepting me with all my faults and believing God has something better for me. And not only that, thanks for helping me to get to where God wants me to be. I love you, Pastor." Jermaine broke down in tears and covered his face with both hands as Pastor Hodges embraced him and prayed a sincere and peaceful prayer. "Thank you so much, Pastor. I really appreciate you!"

"You are very welcome, Jermaine. Remember, I am here for you anytime. Now let's get back to business."

"Yes, Pastor," Jermaine replied. He smiled and raised an eyebrow and thought about how quickly the subject was changed.

"Okay, Son. The armor-bearers meet every first Monday, and the deacons meet every third Thursday. There are two books you must read: Protecting Your Pastor Through It All by Ali Rushnow and The Eyes of the Church by C. M. Ross. They are very short books, but they contain a lot of valuable information that will help you to be a better man for your church, your daughter, and your wife when that time comes." Pastor Hodges had a big smile on his face.

"Yes, Pastor. I will go pick those up tomorrow."

"Son, you can go and get them this evening in the bookstore if you like. I already checked, and we do have them available."

"I sure will. Thanks, Pastor."

"Okay, Jermaine. The last thing I have for you is to meet the armor-bearers and the deacons. We have all been praying for you, and we are all excited to have you come aboard."

"Wow, Pastor, I think this is the best day of my life aside from when Raquel was born! I can't forget my baby." Jermaine chuckled a little.

Pastor Hodges got on his speaker phone and requested that Aubrey send over all the deacons and armor-bearers, who were waiting down the hall in their lounge.

Jermaine never realized how many deacons and armor-bearers Pastor Hodges had until they all flooded his office. Right along with all of Pastor Hodges's armor-bearers was Shela, First Lady Hodges, and all her armor-bearers. It was like a mini reunion, and Jermaine felt like a king.

6

"Oh, I don't feel so well," Raquel said.

"What's wrong?" Martine asked.

"My head is dizzy, and my stomach feels like I got butterflies".

"Let's go to the nurse," Delila said.

"Okay, but let me go into the bathroom first. I think I need to use it," Raquel said. Raquel was walking slowly, holding her head with one hand and placing her other hand on her hip. Martine and Delila were also helping her walk down the hall to the bathroom. As Raquel got into the bathroom and almost into the stall, she passed out on the floor, bumping her shoulder on the way down.

"Oh my God!" Martine screamed. "I'm going to get the nurse." Martine ran down the hall quickly and hysterically. With her hands on the sides of her head, she shouted, "Nurse Howell, help! Nurse Howell!" Teachers were looking out of their classroom doors to see what might be going on. Martine kept running until she got into the nurse's office.

"Nurse Howell! Nurse Howell!"

"Calm down, Martine! What is it?"

"It's Raquel. She was feeling sick and we went into the bathroom and she passed out on the floor!"

"Let's hurry down to the bathroom! Which one?" Nurse Howell got on her walkie talkie and called for Officer Duncan and Officer Hodges.

"In the 200 hall."

"Raquel! Raquel!" Delila said as she splashed water in Raquel's face. "Wake up! Lord, please bless my friend and heal her quickly."

"Hey, what's going on?" Raquel asked, as she popped up off the floor suddenly. "What is going on?"

"You passed out, Raquel! That's what's going on." Delila had a surprised, but evil look on her face.

"I passed out? Oh my God! I passed out?" Raquel looked in the mirror to check her hair.

Nurse Howell, Officer Hodges, and Officer Duncan ran into the bathroom to find Raquel and Delila standing there talking.

"What is going on in here?" Nurse Howell said, pointing her finger. "Is this some type of game you are playing? Because it is not, in any way, shape, or form, funny."

"No, Nurse Howell. Raquel passed out. She just woke back up," Delila said, rolling her eyes.

"Are you okay, Raquel?" Nurse Howell said very sarcastically. "What is going on with you? Why would you be passed out? Did you eat breakfast this morning?"

"I'm fine, Nurse Howell. I really don't know what happened, but I have been feeling very sick lately. And no, I did not eat breakfast this morning."

"Okay, everyone. Follow me to my office so I can check Raquel out really quick and make sure everything is okay." Delila, Raquel, Martine, Officer Hodges, and Officer Duncan all followed Nurse Howell to her office. "Delila and Martine, here let me get you a pass to class. I'll take care of Raquel for you. She is in good hands, girls."

With a look of total disbelief on her face because she knew Nurse Howell, Martine whined, "Nurse Howell, this is our friend. Please, can we stay?"

"Yeah, yeah! I know this is your friend, but I cannot allow you to be out of class, and you know that. You can meet up at lunch or in passing if you don't have any classes together. Here you go, get out! Officer Duncan and Officer Hodges, will you please make sure these two get to class."

"Ugh, I can't stand her," Martine said. That is not fair! Raquel does not need to be in there by herself with that evil old woman. It's going to be like she is on trial or something."

"I know, but she's right, we don't need to be out of class. Besides, we all have next period together."

"You are so shallow, Delila," Martine grumbled. "Whose side are you on here anyways?" Officer Duncan walked Delila to class, and Officer Hodges walked Martine to class.

∞∞∞∞∞∞

"Okay, Raquel, your pulse looks good."

"Thanks."

"Your temperature is kind of high, and so is your blood pressure. Is there anything going on in your life out of the norm?"

"No."

Nurse Howell was a white, sixty-seven-year-old, five-time divorced nurse with no children and no friends. She was very bitter, evil, and judgmental. None of the children in the school liked her, and neither did any of the teachers. She was five feet seven and weighed about 280 pounds. She wore thick glasses, that were so crooked and dirty, on the tip of her nose. She did not wear any denture cream, so her teeth just flopped around all over her mouth. She was utterly disgusting.

"When was your last menstrual period?

"I can't remember exactly! Why? Dang!"

"Have you been having sex?

"No, Ma'am."

"Are you sure? You know how you fast, inner-city teenage girls are, always trying to make your parents into grandparents early. So, you and your boyfriend have not been having sex?"

"No, Ma'am. I said no once, and I don't appreciate that statement, you evil, old, gray-haired snake in the grass. And get some new glasses. Those raggedy, taped-up, crooked, dirty, and cheap wired things look ridiculous." Raquel stormed out of the office with tears in her eyes.

"I hate that lady. I don't have a boyfriend, and why would I want my dad to be a grandparent? Why would she say that? She does not know my situation! She does not see what I have to go through! I am so mad right now! Where are my friends? I need them right now. Raquel was highly upset, and she could not

contain her anger. She walked outside to cool off and give herself some time to get her mind right."

∞∞∞∞∞∞

"Barbecue chicken, macaroni and cheese, green beans, peaches, and juice for lunch! I am loving it," Martine said.

"I know, right?" Delila said. "I love it when we have the good stuff. You sure you don't want to eat, Raquel?"

"I'm sure. I just don't feel well today, and I have a lot on my mind."

"What did the nurse say?" Delila asked.

"Nothing really."

"She said something to make you upset. I can tell," said Delila.

"She just started talking about me like I'm a bad kid and stuff. I'm a good kid, and I try so hard to do the right thing!"

"I know you are not going to allow Funky Fat Howell to get to you with her nasty self and her dirty glasses," Martine said.

"Well, Raquel, let's be real. What do you think is wrong with you?" Delila asked. "I've known you forever, and this has never happened."

"I really don't know, Delila. I'm just going to go to the doctor, that's all."

"Well, there's a pregnancy center up the street," Delila replied, "and pregnancy tests are free! As far as I know you and Diante never had sex, however, I do remember when you were in love with him! Now, I'm not saying you did have sex or that you're pregnant, but I remember when my mom was pregnant with my youngest sister, she used to pass out every month and be dizzy and nauseous."

"I did not have sex with Diante, and I am not just out here having sex, but I think I will go to that center. Please don't ask me any questions, guys. Just take me there and be my support system."

Delila and Martine were very quiet and continued to eat their lunch. They had no clue that Raquel had been having sex, and they had no idea who she would be having sex with. She was interested in a lot of guys, but she was never that interested, as far as they knew.

7

Right after school was over, Delila and Martine walked Raquel to the pregnancy center up the street. There it was: the little brick building on the corner. As Delila and Martine walked through the door, Raquel followed closely behind. With a face that showed total embarrassment, Raquel looked around at everyone, hoping she did not know anyone there.

"Ladies, can I help you?" Asked the young lady at the front desk behind the glass wearing a blue scrub shirt that had baby bottles, pacifiers, diapers, and little baby faces on it.

"Yes, Ma'am. My friend is here to see a doctor," Delila said, pointing toward Raquel.

"Okay, can you please sign in? And here is a packet for her to fill out."

"Alright. Thanks, Ma'am." Delila signed in, grabbed the packet, and went to sit down.

"You are welcome, Sweetie."

Delila proceeded to fill out as much of the packet as she could before she handed it to Raquel to finish answering all the other questions and sign the form. As soon as Raquel had the form fully complete, Martine grabbed it and took it back up to the front desk. Delila leaned over to the end table right beside Raquel and grabbed three magazines for them.

"Raquel Riley."

"Here I am."

"You can come back with me, Sweetie."

"Okay, thanks. Here I come. I'll be back, guys."

"Hello, Raquel. I am Denna Brown. I am a Medical Assistant, and I will be obtaining all your information for the nurse. You can have a seat on the bed or in the chair."

"Okay, thanks," Raquel said as she sat down in the big blue chair that was right next to a big chart that read "Are you pregnant? Prenatal pills are a vital part of your baby's health!" That little bit of information scared Raquel because she had no clue what prenatal pills were or how to get them.

"So what brings you here today, Raquel?"

"I need to take a test."

"What kind of test?"

"A pregnancy test." *This is so embarrassing*, Raquel thought.

"Okay, Sweetie. When was your last menstrual period?"

"I am not sure exactly."

"You're not sure?"

"No, Ma'am.

"How old are you?"

"I just turned fifteen."

"Do you have a boyfriend?"

"No."

"But you believe you may be pregnant?"

"Yes."

"Have you been having sexual intercourse?"

"Not really, but yes, I did."

"So, you have had sex."

"Ma'am, I can't really go into all the details like you want, but the answer to your question is yes. I have had sex once before in my life."

"Was this with your consent?"

"Umm." Raquel looked down at her fumbling hands.

"Yes, Raquel?" Denna said, standing up and reaching out for Raquel's shoulder.

"Well..."

"Raquel, is this uncomfortable for you?"

"Yes, Ma'am. This is very uncomfortable, and no, the sexual contact was not something I agreed to." Raquel took a deep breath and continued looking at the ground. *Why is this happening to me?* She thought to herself.

"So were you raped?"

"What? No ma'am, I...Nevermind. I don't want to call it rape. Please, can we stop talking about this." Tears filled Raquel's eyes and fell down her cheeks.

"I'm sorry, Sweetie." Denna reached over and got a tissue to hand to Raquel. "I have to ask these questions. If you choose not to answer, that is fine. What I want you to do, Raquel, is take this cup into the bathroom right across the hall and urinate in it. Use this wipe and clean the area first. Then I want you to bring the cup back in here and put it on top of this paper towel. I will get your temperature, blood pressure, and pulse as soon as you are finished."

"Yes, Ma'am." Raquel took the cup and the wipes and went into the bathroom and did just as she was instructed. When she got back to the room, she set the cup on the paper towel and sat back down. As she looked around on the wall, she saw another poster that was headed "Choices." Under the heading, the three choices a pregnant woman had were listed: (1) have a baby and keep it, (2) adoption, and (3) abortion. Until Denna returned, Raquel sat there shaking her head in total disappointment as she thought about her situation.

"Okay, Sweetie", Denna said as she walked back through the door. "Let me take this urine sample back across the hall so we can start the testing while I am working on this other stuff. I will be right back."

I am not killing my baby, Raquel thought as soon as Denna stepped back out of the room. *I really hope these people do not try to talk me into that either because I will go off.*

Denna walked back into the room and checked Raquel's blood pressure, temperature, and pulse. When she finished, she let Raquel know all of them were a little high but not too bad. She then continued to ask Raquel questions.

"Have you been feeling ill?"

"Yes, I have been feeling very sick. As a matter of fact, I passed out at school today."

"Wow, Raquel! You passed out at school? Did you talk to anyone?"

"Yes, I spoke with evil old funky Nurse Howell, and she was no help at all."

"Old Nurse Howell. I see she has not changed a bit. Have you been taking anything?"

"No. So you know Nurse Howell?"

"Yes, Sweetie. Everyone knows that bitter old beast. Don't worry about her. Just pray for her. God is the only one who can help that woman," Denna said, as she gave Raquel a comforting smile. For the first time that day, Raquel smiled too.

"Okay, Raquel. Let me go check the pregnancy test."

"Okay." The sound of the word pregnancy made Raquel cringe. She could not believe it. Nervously, she started reading the sign about the prenatal vitamins again, and it started to scare her even more.

"Raquel," Denna said as she entered the room. "Your pregnancy test is positive. Since you do not have a date of your last menstrual period, the nurse is going to come in and do an ultrasound so we can get the exact due date for you. After the ultrasound, Counselor Elaine is going to talk to you about your options."

The word "options" took Raquel back to the word "abortion" on the poster, and she was very quiet as she tried to take this all in. Suddenly, she broke out in tears, crying like a baby. Denna reached out and hugged her and said a comforting prayer that brought so much peace to Raquel.

"Lord, I thank you for who you are, and I pray that you would touch Raquel right now. Give her peace right now, Lord. Encourage her, Lord. Let her know everything is going to be alright. You have got her in the palm of your hand, and you are making her to be more like you. She is a child of the most holy God. She is highly favored. She has been separated for such a time as this. She will be a positive example to her family and her peers. Touch her baby, Lord, so that it will grow up to be the child of God you have ordained it to be. Give this young lady strength to endure. She can make it. I believe you, God, and I am fully persuaded that she will make it with your help. I thank you for who you are, in Jesus's most holy name, Amen."

"Thank you so much, Ms. Denna. I needed that prayer, and I really appreciate it. Can you go and get Martine and Delila now?"

"Of course, I can." Denna reached for the tissue and wiped Raquel's tears.

"Oh my God, what am I going to do? There is really a baby inside of me, and it is not going to disappear like I have been thinking for all these months." Raquel was getting her composure together before her friends walked in the door.

"Hey, Raquel," Delila and Martine said as they stepped into the room.

"Hey, y'all."

"So?" Martine said.

"So I'm pregnant, guys." Raquel looked down at the ground in shame, wondering what evil things Delila was going to say next.

"You're pregnant?" Delila said. "Raquel, I'm going to be an auntie. I know I should not be happy, but I am."

"A new baby? Wow!" Martine said. "Why couldn't it be me? Raquel, you are so special. That is such a blessing."

"Wow! Is it?" Raquel said. "Delila, you are happy for me? I just knew you were going to come in here and treat me like Nurse Howell did earlier. And, Martine, you really don't know what you are saying. But right now, I am going to leave that alone."

"Raquel, I am sorry that I come off like that normally," Delila said, "but I am so happy for you. You don't need to tell me your situation or anything, but I got your back. If there's anything you need, Girl, I got you."

"Thank you, guys, so much. This really helps me because I was trying to figure out what I was going to do, but I have made up my mind. I'm keeping my baby, and I refuse to allow anyone to steer me any other way."

There was a knock on the door, and Denna walked in holding a gown. "Raquel, I'm going to need for you to get undressed and put this gown on with the back open and lay on the bed for your ultrasound."

"Ultrasound? Oh my God," Delila said. "I always wanted to see an ultrasound. When my mom had my baby sister, she had one, and I did not get to go. Oh, Raquel, they can tell you what you are having."

41

"They can?" Raquel and Martine asked in unison.

"Yes, but you have to be kind of far along."

"You, guys, I'm pregnant, I'm fifteen years old, and I don't even have a boyfriend. Are we really supposed to be happy?"

"Should we commit suicide?" Delila said. "Being happy is better than being depressed. Let's look forward to the coming of my niece or nephew. I can think of a million reasons why we should be mad, sad, or upset, but I'd rather choose to be happy. You feel me?"

"I guess you are right, cause before you guys came in here, I was crying hard. The poster says 'adoption' or 'abortion' and that is all I could think of. And then that over there is talking about prenatal vitamins. What is that?"

"First of all, I know you were not considering abortion or adoption," Martine exclaimed.

"I mean, if you are going to carry a baby for nine months, why give it away? Come on now, Raquel," said Delila.

"It's not that I was considering any of it, but I saw it, and it makes you think."

Ms. Denna walked back into the room followed by a lady in a white lab coat.

"Hello, ladies. I am Pascha Holbert, your radiologist." After getting all her tools in place and ensuring that Raquel was comfortable, she went to work.

"Raquel, I am going to insert this wand into your vagina. It will give us all the information for your baby." Thankfully, the baby had all its fingers and toes, the heart was perfect, and so were the lungs and brain.

"Would you like to know what you are having?" Pascha asked.

"Yes, I would," all three girls said in unison.

"Okay, look. See, the legs are opened. You are having a baby girl. She is very healthy, Raquel, and you are moving along great in your pregnancy. From the looks of it, your due date is February 26. It shows you are about 21 weeks pregnant."

"A girl? February 26? Wow!" Raquel said.

"Wow!" Delila and Martine said.

"Raquel, I am going to give you this copy of your ultrasound so you can show all your family and friends."

"Really?"

"Really, Raquel. Here you go."

"Thank you so much."

"Ladies, it was so nice to meet you. Raquel, take good care of yourself and your baby."

"Yes, Ma'am," the three of them said.

"Raquel, now you can go ahead and get dressed," Ms. Denna said. "When you are done, come down the hall and go to the first office on the left. Counselor Elaine T., is ready when you are."

Raquel got dressed as she and her friends chatted about the new baby girl that was soon coming. When she finished, she, Martine, and Delila went down the hall to the counselor's office.

"Hello, ladies, come in. I am Counselor Elaine T. Which one of you is Raquel?"

"Me. Hello!"

"Hello, I am Martine."

"Hello, I am Delila."

"Raquel, you want these ladies here for your consultation?"

"Yes, I do. They are my support system. I trust them."

"That's fine, Sweetie. So, Raquel, you are five months pregnant. How do you feel?"

"Well, before I came here, I felt terrible. But since I have been here, my mind is freer, and I feel a lot more comfortable."

"What are your plans?"

"I plan on having my baby."

"Okay, Sweetie. So, you believe you can raise a baby?"

"Yes, I believe I can do it. I have my friends, my dad, and his girlfriend. I am very confident that I will be able to do this."

"That is very positive and mature of you, Raquel."

"Thanks."

"So, abortion and adoption are out for you, right?"

"Those are not options for me at all, and I refuse to even go into detail about either of them."

"Denna had some concerns about your situation. Is it okay to discuss that now?

"Yes, Ma'am."

"She believes you were raped."

"I told her I was not raped."

"Will you be able to talk to your child's father?"

"Umm, I believe so."

"Okay. Are you going to let your father know?"

"Eventually."

"Sweetie, he will need to be informed soon. Your baby is extremely healthy for you to have had no medical attention, but you will need to get to a doctor as soon as possible for regular visits."

"Can I just come here?"

"Yes, Sweetie, you can do that."

"What are prenatal vitamins?"

"They are vitamins given to expecting mothers that have all the nutrients you and your baby need."

"Okay. Can you give me those?"

"Yes, I can, Sweetie, if you are going to come here. Does your father have insurance for you? If not, I can help you sign up for Medicaid. If you need anything from me, here is my card. Call me on my cell phone at any time. And for the record, anything we discuss is confidential. If you need help telling your family, let me know because I can and will help you."

"I appreciate you, Counselor Elaine T. I need someone to talk to sometimes. I mean, I got my girls, and they always got my back, but I can't keep burdening them with my issues. I am not sure if my father has insurance, but I will find out."

"Alright, Sweetie! I want to see you back in two weeks. Ask Denna to give you a bottle of the vitamins on your way out. Thanks for your time. It was nice to meet you ladies. Be good and take care."

Raquel got her vitamins on the way out the door. As they walked home, Delila and Martine asked her how she was going to break the news to her father. She was very unsure how, but she knew she was definitely going to have to tell him soon.

8

Shela was expecting her wonderful man, Jermaine Marquice Riley III, so when the doorbell rang she happily ran over and looked out the peephole. Yes, just as she expected; it was him.

"Good morning, Beautiful. How is my lady this morning?"

"Baby, I want to be wonderful, but I am really not feeling so well." Shela held her stomach with her right hand, and she had a small frown on her face.

"Well, you look great." Jermaine reached out and grabbed Shela's left hand to kiss it.

"Baby, I have had an awful morning."

"Well, what's wrong, Love? You need me to step out and get you some medicine or something?"

"What I might need for you to do is to step out and get me a pregnancy test." She looked Jermaine straight in his eyes with a serious look on her face, unsure what his reply would be.

"Baby, are you serious? I'm so sorry! This is my fault. I was not trying to—"

"Jermaine, the one thing I have always wanted is a baby. I prayed to God to send a man who was looking for his good thing so he could find me, and we could be fruitful and multiply. This would be a dream come true. I am not mad, Baby, I am so happy, excited, and delighted."

"Wow, Love. You have got to be kidding me. I always wanted another baby too, but I did not want it to be out of wedlock. Pastor and First Lady are not going to approve of this."

"And? We did not do this on purpose. It happened, and that's that," Shela said with her lips curled and her finger pointing in the air. "My Pastor and the First Lady are not that shallow anyways."

"Girl, you are something amazing. Thank you so much for having my baby. I love you so much, Shela. When God blessed me with you, he was really showing off. He gave me a supreme gift, and I would not exchange it for anything in the world. This could be little Jermaine, but if it's little Shermaine, that's okay too."

"Shermaine? Where did you get that from?"

"Baby, that's Shela and Jermaine put together. What do you think?"

"I think it's absolutely perfect, Baby. I love it."

"I love you, Shela." Jermaine embraced her from the back and rubbed her belly with a look of happiness on his face.

"I love you too, Jermaine, and thank you for being so wonderful, Baby."

"Alright, Babe. I have got to get out of here. I was just bringing your breakfast and lunch. I'll buy the test when I get off work, and we'll do a special candlelight dinner to celebrate."

"The breakfast smells wonderful. I will try my best to eat it all. But a candlelight dinner? Baby, what are we celebrating?"

"Our love and our new baby, Shela." Jermaine kissed Shela on the forehead and gave her a big hug.

"I need to go finish getting myself together anyways. I love you, Baby."

"I love you too, Shela, and I want you in my life forever. I'll call you on my lunch."

After Jermaine left, Shela began to praise and worship God for his goodness. "Lord, I thank you. You have been so good to me. A good man, with a beautiful daughter, and a new baby of my own. I never thought Jermaine would react like that or I would have told him months ago. He really does love me, doesn't he, Lord? What did I do to deserve all this greatness? I guess the saying is true: 'favor just ain't fair.'"

∞∞∞∞∞∞

On the way to Shela's house, Jermaine stopped at the neighborhood Walmart to pick up a couple of pregnancy tests for Shela and a couple of bottles of sparkling grape juice. Then he made his way to the Olive Garden to pick up the shrimp alfredo and breadsticks—Shela and Raquel's favorite food. After that, he went by his house to pick up Raquel.

When Shela opened the door, she greeted Jermaine and Raquel with a hug. They walked into the formal dining room where Shela had it set up beautifully. The candles lit the room up just right.

"Wow, Shela!" Raquel said. "What is the special occasion? This looks beautiful."

"We'll explain in a few minutes, Honey," Jermaine said.

"Okay, Dad."

"Let me set up the food, y'all," Jermaine said. "Here is your package, Babe. Go do your thing."

With a great big smile and both of her deep dimples showing, Shela grabbed the bag. Jermaine kissed her on her forehead, and she skipped away, swinging the bag.

While Shela was handling her business, Jermaine fixed the food neatly on the table and talked to Raquel about her day at school. She told him it was great and went into detail about some of the things that had happened in some of her classes. Then she asked him about his day. Jermaine told Raquel that this was one of the best days of his life. But he let her know for sure that the best day was when he found out she was going to be born and that the next best day was when she was born.

"Yes, yes, yes! Thank you, Jesus," Shela shouted from her bedroom.

"Wow, she's happy, Daddy." Raquel had a huge smile on her face.

"I know. I can't wait to fill you in. You are going to be so excited."

"I am? Really? Did we win the lottery?" Raquel asked with wide eyes and a cheery voice.

"No, Sweetie, not exactly. However, in my eyes, we are darn close." Jermaine folded his hands and twiddled his thumbs. "Happiness is priceless, Raquel."

"Yeah, Daddy, I know. You remind me quite frequently. Dad, I am so thankful that you are happy now. It helps me to be happy. We've been through so much since Mommy passed, but these last four months have been spectacular, for the most part."

"Yes, Baby, I know. Over the last four years, I have not been myself, but God has given me a renewed mind, a new heart, and a new love for him and my family."

"That is great, Daddy." Raquel looked down at the ground, and you could feel the sadness overtaking her.

"Baby, are you okay?"

"I'm fine, Daddy. I've just got a lot on my mind right now."

"Girl, you got bills? You got rent to pay?"

"No, Daddy, but..."

"But what, Raquel?"

"Nothing, Daddy. I'll talk about it later. I'd hate to ruin everyone's good mood."

"Okay, I'm ready to eat, guys," Shela said, as she reentered the room with a big smile on her face. "Let's get this party started."

Jermaine and Shela sat down beside each other, and Raquel sat across from Shela. Jermaine proceeded to say grace, and they all started to dig into their shrimp alfredo and bread sticks. After about thirty minutes of talking and eating, Shela could not wait any longer to give the great news.

"Jermaine, are you ready to share?" Shela asked.

"I am ready when you are, Shela."

"What is it that we are sharing, guys? I am so lost here," Raquel said.

"Can I say it?" Shela asked.

"Of course, you can, Honey."

"Alright already! Please, somebody, say something!" Raquel demanded.

"Raquel, we are having a baby," Shela said.

Raquel's eyes widened, and her right hand cupped her mouth. You could tell she was truly shocked. She was very still and didn't say a word.

"Baby," Jermaine called out. Raquel turned her eyes to look at him, with her hand still cupping her mouth, still not saying a word.

"Are you okay, Raquel?" Shela asked.

Finally, Raquel managed to move her hand and force a smile. "Wow, Dad and Shela. I can't believe it. A baby? Congratulations!" Raquel fumbled and picked up her fork.

"Thanks, Honey!" Jermaine said. "Are you sure you are okay? I mean, I know this is big news, but you seem extra jittery."

"I am just very shocked, but I am okay. I am so excited for you two. I'm going to be a big sister."

"I am going to be a mommy," Shela said.

"I am going to be a daddy again."

Raquel sat there with a smile on her face. Yet she was dying inside. She could not believe it. She thought, *I have to tell my*

*daddy I'm pregnant, and the woman he is in love with is pregnant
too. I could never say it. What am I going to do?*

"I have one more surprise." Jermaine reached into his pocket
and pulled out a small velvet box. "Shela, I love you with all my
heart. I knew the day I met you that you were different. You are
the woman of God the bible talks about. You are truly a blessing
to me and my daughter, Raquel. I don't want to spend another
moment without you being Mrs. Shela Renee Riley. Shela Renee
Johnston, will you marry me?" Jermaine pulled out a two-karat
diamond swish white gold engagement ring.

"Oh my God!" Shela stood up, and her mouth opened wide.
"Jermaine, you're serious, aren't you?"

"Am I serious? Yes, Shela. Love of my life, will you marry me?"

"Yes, I will. Yes, I will," Shela said, fighting back tears.
"Jermaine, all my life I have waited for a man like you, and I am
so thankful that God has answered my prayers." Jermaine reached
up and put the engagement ring on her finger.

Wow, what a day to remember, Raquel thought as she stood up
to hug and congratulate her new stepmother and her father.
"Shela, you are going to be a beautiful bride. Do you think I can
call you mom when you guys get married?"

"Raquel, you can call me mom now. I know I will never take
your biological mother's place, but I will do my best to be a good
mother to you. Wow, what an honor!" Tears started rolling down
Shela's face again.

"Mommy," Raquel said as she and Shela hugged each other. "Please promise to stay in our lives forever, Shela. We really need you."

"Raquel, I promise that there is nothing that will ever make me leave. I promise to fight for whatever it takes to keep my family together forever, and I say that in the name of Jesus."

"What a moment," Jermaine said. "Now let me pour this sparkling grape juice so we can do a toast to our happiness. Jermaine popped the top, and they all gave their own personal encouraging words and tapped their glasses to make the toast official.

"So, Daddy, do you have a date in mind?"

"I am thinking within the next week or two. I would marry my queen tomorrow if I could, but it's all up to you, Shela."

"Wow!" Raquel said.

"It's all up to me?" Shela asked. "'Wow is right, Raquel. Well, Baby, we don't have to have a super big wedding, but I want it to be nice. Well, how about a big reception?"

"Shela, it's your world. Whatever you want is perfectly fine with me. I am going to call the pastor in the morning and see when his schedule is open, and we will go talk to him."

9

Ring, ring.

"Hello, Pastor Hodges speaking."

"Hello, Pastor Hodges. This is Jermaine Riley."

"Jermaine, Son, how's it going?"

"All is well, Pastor. Are you busy?"

"Always." Pastor Hodges chuckled. "What do you need, Son?"

"Shela and I would like to meet with you sometime soon, whenever you have time."

"Well, Jermaine, I am just about to beat Bishop Young in this game of golf. So how about we meet in about two hours? You hungry?"

"Two hours sounds great. And yes, Sir, I am hungry."

"Let's meet up at Applebee's on Seventy-Second and Dodge. See you there in two hours."

"Alright. Good-bye."

"Bye."

∞∞∞∞∞∞

Ring, ring.

"Hey, Babe."

"Hey, Beautiful Mother of My Children. We are going to go and meet up with Pastor at Applebee's on Seventy Second and Dodge in two hours."

"Oh my God, Jermaine! I am so excited, but so afraid."

"It's okay, Shela. We got this. Now I need for you to call your father and see when we can go by there to talk to him."

"Wow! Thanks a lot for leaving that up to me."

"Shela, I'll call him. Give me the number."

"Are you serious?"

"Yes, Ma'am. I love you, girl, and I am so proud of my prize. I will tell anyone, even your father, Mr. Johnston."

"Baby, you are hilarious. The number is 402-318-4280."

"Okay, Sweetie. I'll call you back. Bye."

"See you later."

∞∞∞∞∞∞∞

Ring, ring.

"Hello."

"Hello, Mr. Johnston. This is Jermaine."

"Jermaine, how are you?"

"I am well, Sir. And you?"

"I am great. What's going on?"

"Well, I want to get some of your time. I need to talk to you about a few things."

"Sounds interesting, Jermaine. I will be home all evening. Stop by anytime."

"Thanks a lot. I will definitely be there sometime this evening. See you then."

10

Ring, ring.

"Hello."

"Good afternoon, First Lady."

"Hey, Shela. How are you doing?"

"I am good. I have something to tell you."

"What is it, Lady? You sound so excited."

"Are you sitting down?"

"No, I am washing clothes. Come on, Shela. What is it?"

"Well, Jermaine proposed to me last night."

"Shela, oh my God. It's about time you got hitched, girl. We've all been waiting for this moment for years."

"I know, First Lady. I am so happy, and I know Jermaine really loves me."

"So, do we have a date?"

"Jermaine wants to do it as soon as possible."

"Shela, are you pregnant?

Shela paused for a few seconds, swallowed hard, and answered. "First Lady, yes I am, but that is not the only reason why."

"Shela!"

"First Lady, it happened once and—"

"So, are we planning a wedding and a baby shower? Girl, I am not mad at you! Shocked but not mad. I am overjoyed for you. God works in mysterious ways, and it is about time you had a

57

family. Now the one you are going to have to get to understand it, is your Pastor."

"We are meeting with Pastor in a couple of hours at Applebee's."

"On Seventy-Second Street?"

"Yes."

"Am I welcome to come?"

"Of course, but please don't tell Pastor what the meeting is about. Jermaine would like to do it."

"Shela, I won't say a word. I'm going to call him now so he can tell me about the meeting, and I can invite myself," First Lady Hodges said, laughing.

"First Lady, that is why I love you so much. You are so real and so understanding."

"Alright. See you in a couple of hours. Bye."

"See you."

11

Jermaine had gone by to pick up Shela, and they arrived at Applebee's about thirty minutes early. They were sitting there laughing and talking when they saw Pastor and First Lady Hodges being escorted to the table. Jermaine stood up to hug the First Lady and shake Pastor Hodges's hand. Shela stood up to give both of them a hug. The waiter came by to take their drink orders, and they all began talking.

"So, Pastor, did you enjoy your golf game today?" Jermaine asked.

"Yes, it was wonderful. This was the first time I actually beat Bishop Young." Pastor Hodges had a big smile on his face.

"Oh, really?"

They all began laughing.

"And First Lady Hodges," Jermaine said, "How are you?"

"I am well, happy, and excited."

The waiter returned with their drinks. After placing each drink in front of the appropriate person, he took their entrée orders.

"Jermaine, you sounded so excited on the phone. I could tell you really needed to talk."

"Yes, Sir," Jermaine replied.

"Okay, so what brings us all together?" Pastor Hodges asked. First Lady looked over at Shela, and they smiled and winked at one another.

"Pastor, I proposed to Shela last night. She is now my fiancé," Jermaine proudly exclaimed.

"Shela!" Pastor called out with much authority. "So that is why you are hiding your hand."

"Well, Pastor, I wanted to wait until Jermaine told you," Shela had a beautiful smile on her face.

"That is awesome. And that ring is beautiful. I see you don't come cheap, huh, Son?"

"I want the best for my wife," Jermaine replied.

"Congratulations to the two of you," First Lady Hodges said. "This is great. Jermaine, I hope you understand what a jewel you have here."

"Yes, congratulations! And my wife is exactly right. God has blessed you with a gem."

"Thanks a lot, you two," Shela said.

"Thanks so much. I truly understand this woman's worth. I know God has smiled upon her and that she is an enormous blessing in my life. I promise to always treat her like the queen she is."

"Alright, Son," Pastor Hodges said. He had a proud smile on his face because he was truly happy for his daughter in Christ.

The waiter returned with everyone's entrée, and the food looked fabulous. Pastor Hodges asked Jermaine to do the honors and pray over the food and without hesitation; Jermaine accepted the honor.

"Lord, we thank you for bringing us here and for this food we are about to eat. We pray this food will bring nourishment to our bodies and that you will bless the hands that prepared the food and that it would bring no hurt, harm, or danger. We thank you in Jesus's name, Amen."

As everyone was eating, talking, laughing, and enjoying their food, Jermaine interrupted the conversation. "There is one more thing, Pastor."

"Yes, Son?" Pastor Hodges put down his fork and crossed his hands, patiently waiting to hear what Jermaine wanted to share next.

"Well, Pastor"—Jermaine took a deep breath— "Shela and I are having a baby."

The table was extremely silent for about a minute as Pastor Hodges looked Jermaine right in the eyes, being sure not to blink or take his eyes off him.

"Honey, are you okay?" First Lady Hodges asked.

"Pastor, are you alright?" Shela asked.

"I am fine, everyone. I am very shocked and surprised, but I am just fine." Pastor Hodges picked up his fork and continued eating his food while staring from Shela to Jermaine and then to First Lady. "So, when did you find this out, Son?"

"Last night," Shela and Jermaine replied nervously.

"When did this happen, Jermaine?" Pastor Hodges asked.

"Pastor, yes it was my fault. That was about three and a half or four months ago, and it only happened once. I know that does not matter, but—"

"So, Shela, you are about four months pregnant, right?" Pastor Hodges asked.

"Yes, Pastor."

"Well, I guess we are going to have a baby and a wedding, right?"

"Right!" Jermaine, Shela, and First Lady Hodges said.

"So why are you all looking at me like I'm crazy? What are you expecting me to do? Wrong is wrong, and you two are definitely out of the will of God, but I am not going to and have no right to judge either of you. I know that none of us is perfect, and there are times when temptation overtakes us. I am not okaying your actions, and you will be dealt with accordingly! On the other hand, congratulations to the both of you on your new baby and your wedding. I am sincerely happy for the two of you. Shela, it is about time," Pastor Hodges said with a big smile on his face as he stood up to shake Jermaine's hand and give Shela another hug.

When the waiter brought the ticket, Jermaine tried to pay the tab, but Pastor and First Lady Hodges insisted they pay so they could bless the new couple. Plus, they reminded them that they would need all their money. They all laughed and hugged and walked away together.

12

"Come on in, guys. How are you doing?" Mrs. Johnston, Shela's mother, said as she gave Shela and Jermaine a hug.

"We are well," Shela and Jermaine replied together.

"To what do we give this honor? You hardly ever come by, now that you have Mr. Jermaine in your life." Mrs. Johnston laughed.

"Mom," Shela said with a smile on her face.

"Well, Mrs. Johnston, I talked to Mr. Johnston earlier, and he said I could stop by," Jermaine replied.

"Okay, come back here. He is in the living room watching television."

Jermaine and Shela followed Mrs. Johnston back to the living room. As they entered, Mr. Johnston stood up to greet them properly.

"Hey, Daddy," Shela hugged her father.

"How's my girl?"

"Wonderful, Daddy. And you?"

"I am well, Hun. Jermaine, you sounded like you had some urgent news. Is everything okay?"

"Yes, Sir. I just need to talk. Everything is well." Jermaine replied, scratching his head.

"Alone or all together?"

"All together," Shela replied, before Jermaine could get anything out.

"Okay. Let's get it started. Let me pause this television. I am excited to see what it is we are going to talk about," Mr. Johnston said.

"First of all, Mr. Johnston, I proposed to Shela last night. I truly love her, and I am making her my wife."

"Hallelujah," Mrs. Johnston said with a great big smile on her face and both of her hands lifted to the air. "My baby is getting married. Congratulations, Shela." Mrs. Johnston was very happy, and it showed. She stood up and hugged Shela and Jermaine and then thanked him for being so good to her daughter.

"Well, bless the Lord, Jermaine. Let me see that rock, Baby," Mr. Johnston said. "It is absolutely beautiful, Jermaine. You don't play, do you? I know for sure this here ring cost a pretty penny."

Proudly, Jermaine said, "Yes, Sir, but I only want the best for the best."

Everyone smiled with great excitement and adored Shela's beautiful ring.

"Have we set a date?" Mr. Johnston asked.

"I really don't want to wait, Mr. Johnston. I am thinking within the next couple of weeks."

"That's rushing it a bit, isn't it?"

"Not really. Why wait? I know I love her, and I know she is my good thing."

"Okay. Well, that's a good way to shut me up." Mr. Johnston replied, and everyone began to laugh.

"Mr. and Mrs. Johnston, there is one more thing," Jermaine said, grasping his hands tightly while twiddling his thumbs.

"Wow, something else? What is it?" Mr. Johnston asked.

"Shela and I"—Jermaine took a very deep breath— "are having a baby."

"So there is a reason for the rush," Mr. Johnston replied.

"No, Sir," Jermaine blurted out. "I assure you, whether Shela was having my baby or not, I would still marry her. I love her, and I have never known a love like this before. My daughter loves her, and I want to spend the rest of my life with her."

"Jermaine," Mrs. Johnston said, "I can feel your sincerity. Honey, let's be real. When you proposed to me, I was pregnant too, but our baby did not make it to full term."

"Wow! Are you really going to put me out there like that, Dear?"

"Honey, I am just saying. I want them to know it happens and to not be ashamed of love."

"You are right, Babe," Mr. Johnston replied.

"Mom, you never told me that. Wow! That is new news," Shela said with a shocked look on her face and pointing to her mother and father, with a smile on her face.

As everyone continued to talk and laugh, Mr. Johnston said, "I guess we've got a wedding and a baby shower to plan!"

"This is so exciting to me," Mrs. Johnston said, with her hand on her hip and a big smile on her face. We have been praying for a good husband for Shela for years, Jermaine, and you came right on time. Now I am going to have two grandchildren!"

13

Everything was set up beautifully, starting with the hot pink carpet that sat under the chocolate-colored iron plant stands. These plant stands stood directly across from each other in front of the middle aisles in the center of the sanctuary. Freshly cut hot pink roses were neatly laid on the flat surface at the top of the plant stand. The unity candle was five inches thick and three feet high and sat inside a beautiful chocolate-colored candleholder. Truly Blessed, the quartet, sat behind the pulpit where the choir usually sang. They played beautiful music on their stringed instruments.

As the music played, Pastor Hodges and Jermaine entered from the doors directly behind the pulpit. Right on cue, Tiara, Shela's maid of honor, and Big Blue, Jermaine's best man, came down the aisle, arm in arm perfectly. Then they split off, Tiara to the left and Big Blue to the right.

Next the bride's maids and groomsmen came down the aisle, hand in hand. First came Rochelle and Javon, Shela's friend, and Jermaine's brother from St. Louis. Then came Sharon, another friend of Shela's, and Jarod, Jermaine's other brother from Kansas City.

Jarod's three-year-old son, Marquice, was a handsome little ring bearer and he looked great in his brown suit, carrying his pink pillow. Javon's beautiful five-year-old daughter, Chasity, with her long, thick beautiful candy curls down the middle of her back, was the flower girl. The ushers rolled out the white carpet over the pink carpet, and she gracefully threw out the brown and pink rose petals.

As the back doors opened, Jermaine got a good glimpse of his wife, and tears began to fall from his eyes. You could tell he was excited and proud. Shela's face was beautiful through her lace veil as she stood there, arm in arm with her proud, smiling father. They walked down the aisle. Shela, with her beautiful smile, looked like a million bucks, walking gracefully and with much class. Her strapless all white diamond-embedded dress with her twelve-foot train had her looking just like a queen on her way to the ball.

When they stood firmly at the front, Pastor Hodges asked, "Who gives this woman away?"

"I do!" Mr. Johnston said proudly. Then immediately, Jermaine went down to retrieve his bride and walk her up the steps.

The wedding festivities ran rather quickly and smoothly, and before you knew it, it was time for the big introduction.

"I now introduce to you all, Mr. and Mrs. Riley." Everyone stood up and celebrated this wonderful man and woman on their special day.

Pictures of the wedding party were taken immediately following the ceremony. After dinner, Raquel, Rochelle, and Big Blue gave the initial toast, and the rest of the wedding party followed with their words of encouragement. Shela and Jermaine made sure they went to each table to take pictures with all their guests and to thank each of them for celebrating their special day with them.

At the end of the reception, Jermaine and Shela waved good-bye and were off to catch their flight to Miami so they could make their honeymoon cruise to the Bahamas the following day.

14

"Hello, everyone. Come in. How are you doing?" Mrs. Johnston greeted everyone who came through the door with a hug, while Raquel took time to individually introduce everyone so they could get more acquainted.

"Well, you certainly have a beautiful house," Raquel's Uncle Javon said.

"Thank you very much," Mr. and Mrs. Johnston replied.

The family sat around talking, laughing, and visiting with one another. Raquel's uncles wanted to spend a little time with her before they got back on the road in the morning to go home. Suddenly, Raquel began to look sick in the face, like she was confused.

"Raquel, is everything okay?" Mrs. Johnston asked her, but she got no answer from Raquel. Raquel fell over onto her Uncle Jarod.

"Raquel!" Mrs. Johnston screamed.

"I think she's having a seizure," Uncle Jarod said, trying to shake her to wake her up.

"No, it's not a seizure. She passed out or blacked out, whatever you want to call it. Does this happen often?" Aunt Lisa, Uncle Javon's wife, asked.

"I never heard of it happening," Mrs. Johnston replied.

"Call 911! Let me check her pulse," Aunt Lisa said. "Well, she still has a pulse. Raquel! Raquel!" Aunt Lisa called out with no

70

response. "Mrs. Johnston, can you get me a cold wet towel to rub on her face?"

"Yes, I will be right back."

"I got it, Babe," Mr. Johnston said, rushing to the kitchen to get the towel.

As Aunt Lisa did her best to make sure Raquel was comfortable, she patted her chest lightly, felt her sides, and slightly pushed on her stomach. *Oh my God,* she thought, *Raquel is pregnant. Oh my God!*

"Here's the rag," Mr. Johnston said, handing it down to Aunt Lisa.

"Thanks a lot." Aunt Lisa rubbed it on Raquel's face and called her name again. "Raquel, Raquel!"

Raquel began to open her eyes just as the ambulance pulled up.

"Tell the ambulance we've got it."

"Are you sure? She just woke up. I think she should go to the hospital," Mrs. Johnston said.

"I'm fine." Raquel opened her eyes wide. "What is going on?"

"You passed out," Aunt Lisa said. "How do you feel?"

"Oh my God, not again," Raquel mumbled.

"Let's help her up. Raquel, I want to talk to you alone. Mrs. Johnston, is there a room where we can have some privacy?" Aunt Lisa asked.

"Yes there is. Raquel take her to your room."

"Yes, Ma'am." They walked to the room while everyone sat in the living room, trying to figure out the problem.

"Well, asthma is serious in our family," Uncle Javon said.

"No, I really don't think its asthma, Bro," Uncle Jarod said. "I sure hope she's not pregnant. That was my children's momma's reaction to all our pregnancies.

"Pregnant?" Mrs. Johnston said. "No, I don't think so. She's not having sex. At least I wouldn't think she was. Jermaine has really done a great job with her, and he's not going for that."

∞∞∞∞∞∞

"Raquel, what's going on?" Aunt Lisa asked.

"Huh?" Raquel replied.

"No huh, Raquel!"

"I don't know, Aunt Lisa."

"Raquel, when you were passed out, I felt your stomach. I know you are pregnant. How long have you known this? Have you been to a doctor? Does Jermaine know?"

"No, my dad does not know."

"Raquel, you know better. How far along are you?"

"I am due on February 26."

"February 26? Have you seen a doctor?"

"I have."

"You have? Without Jermaine? Are you taking prenatal vitamins?"

"Yes, Aunt Lisa."

Aunt Lisa hugged Raquel tightly. "Raquel, you've got to talk to your dad."

"I know, Aunt Lisa. But I can't."

"You have no choice, Raquel."

"I was going to, but now they're having their own baby."

"I'll tell them."

"No, Aunt Lisa!"

"Tell Shela's mother," Aunt Lisa suggested. "Talk to her, and then she can help you tell your dad and Shela. I'm going to call her in here, and we'll talk to her together."

"Oh my God! Lord, why me?" Raquel asked.

Aunt Lisa cracked the door open a little. "Mrs. Johnston," she hollered down the hall, "Mrs. Johnston, please come here."

"Yes, Hun! Yes, here I come." Mrs. Johnston walked into the room and closed the door slowly behind her. "What is going on? Are you okay, Raquel?"

"I'm fine, Grandma," Raquel replied, looking down at the ground.

"You don't look fine."

"You want me to tell her, Raquel?" Aunt Lisa asked.

"Yes, Ma'am." Raquel reached for her stomach and ran suddenly to her bathroom to throw up.

"Mrs. Johnston, Raquel is pregnant."

"Oh my God! She's pregnant? I just told them there was no way Raquel was pregnant. I can't believe it. Raquel, are you alright?"

"Yes, Ma'am." Raquel continued to throw up.

"How do you know for sure?" Mrs. Johnston asked.

"Well, this is what happens sometimes when women get pregnant. But when I was examining her after she passed out, I tried to push down on her stomach, and I noticed a bulge."

"Oh my God!" Mrs. Johnston whispered. "Shela and Raquel are both having a baby. Jermaine is going to kill that girl."

After brushing her teeth, Raquel came back into the room and sat right next to Mrs. Johnston.

"Raquel, I love you," Mrs. Johnston said. "I want you to know we all do things that maybe we regret, but I assure you that a baby is a blessing from God." Mrs. Johnston reached over and hugged Raquel, and Raquel began to cry.

"Grandma, I am so scared. I did not mean for this to happen. I don't know why this happened to me."

"Raquel, it's okay," Mrs. Johnston said. "Everything happens for a reason. God is still in control, and he allowed this. You never know what the Lord is trying to do, but I assure you there is a good reason, and eventually He will reveal it to you."

"Amen to that," Aunt Lisa said. "Hold on to those words, Raquel, and know it is the honest-to-God truth. I mean, I am not condoning it, but your uncle and I had our first child at sixteen, so, it does happen, and life goes on."

"Thanks," Raquel said as she wiped her face. "So, Grandma, can you help me tell Dad and Mom when they come back? And Aunt Lisa, please don't tell anyone. I want to make sure Dad and Shela know before the rest of the family."

"You got it, Raquel," Aunt Lisa responded.

Raquel got her composure back, and they all walked back into the living room together.

Jermaine's family members left early in the morning and had a safe trip back home.

15

"Jermaine, this was the most wonderful vacation ever," Shela said. "This honeymoon was perfect. You are just too good to be true." She reached over and kissed Jermaine on the cheek and grabbed his hand and held it.

"Baby, it was spectacular. My rib, my helpmate, my equal, the love of my life, my beautiful wife, I love you so much."

"Well, let's go by your old place to make sure everything is moved out. That was so nice of you to give all your furniture to Ms. Hall and her children."

"I know how it is to need and struggle and be single, so I figured I should give it to someone single."

"A good man is so hard to find but thank God you found me. I love you too, Jermaine."

When they got to Jermaine's old place, they saw that Rent-A-Brother had cleaned the apartment so good that it looked like new.

"Alright now, let's ride by our house," Shela said, "so we can make sure it looks like it's supposed to."

"You've got it, Babe."

They drove up to the house and went inside.

"Okay," Shela said, "Raquel's room looks good. I see all her stuff is in the closet, and her boxes are on the floor.

"Yep, yep," Jermaine replied. "And all my stuff is here in this extra room. I will be sure to get this all cleaned up and fixed up soon, Baby."

"Jermaine, don't act like that." Shela reached over and kissed her husband. "It's all good." They continued to walk through the house and prepared to leave.

"The keys are on the counter. I am so thankful Daddy came over here and opened the door for us and set the alarm," Shela said.

"How's my baby doing today, Shela? Is it moving around again? That was an amazing feeling."

"It's fine, Honey, I can't wait until the end of the week so we can go find out what we are having."

"Yeah, I know. I can't wait either. Alright, Shela, let's get over to your parents' house to retrieve our child."

16

Knock, knock!

"It's us! It's Mommy and Daddy," Jermaine said through the door.

"Hello, guys," Mr. Johnston said as he opened the door to let Shela and Jermaine in. "How was the trip? How are the newlyweds?"

"We are well, Sir, and I am happy as ever," Jermaine replied.

"I am great, Dad. Happy to be home with my husband," Shela said with a proud look on her face.

"Daddy and Mommy," Raquel said as she ran and jumped into her dad's arms. "I missed you so much."

"We missed you too, Baby," Shela said.

"Hey, guys," Mrs. Johnston said. "How was everything?"

"It was great, Mom," Shela replied. "It just can't get any better than this. God is good. Mom, our cruise was amazing!"

"Wonderful, you two," Mrs. Johnston said. "Let's sit down and talk a little bit.

"Okay, I'm going to go out to work in the garage while you guys talk," Mr. Johnston said, because he did not like being involved in any mess.

"Maybe I should go with you," Jermaine said.

"No, no, Jermaine, please stay," Mrs. Johnston asked. They all walked back to the dining room and sat at the table.

"What is going on, Mom?" Shela asked. "I can tell you've got something to say. It's bad news, isn't it? Oh my God, I knew it. Things were going way too well."

"Calm down, Shela. It's fine," Mrs. Johnston said.

"Jermaine, Baby, something is wrong. Anytime Mom wants to talk and Dad leaves the room, something happened," Shela explained.

"Raquel, is everything okay," Jermaine asked with a suspicious look on his face.

"Yes," Raquel answered, looking down and making no eye contact.

"Well, Jermaine and Shela, I am so glad your trip went well. However, we had a situation when you guys were away," Mrs. Johnston said.

"A situation?" Shela and Jermaine asked.

"A situation!" Mrs. Johnston answered. "Raquel passed out in the living room on the couch when your family stopped by to visit." She pointed her hand at Jermaine.

"She passed out?" Jermaine asked, turning toward Raquel. "Are you okay, Baby?"

"Well, Jermaine, Raquel is pregnant."

"What? Pregnant? Are you kidding me? How could you do this Raquel?"

"Dad, I am so sorry."

"You're sorry? And that fixes what? Is that it?" Jermaine hollered.

"Jermaine, calm down," Mrs. Johnston said.

"Calm down, Mrs. Johnston? My fifteen-year-old daughter is pregnant, and I am supposed to calm down? I have done everything for this girl, and now that I have a wife and I am about to have a baby, I am going to have a grandchild too. No! Raquel how could you do this?"

"Dad, I am so sorry!" Raquel pleaded with tears streaming down her face.

"You're sorry?" Jermaine stood up and grabbed his head with both hands.

"Jermaine! Stop it!" Shela yelled, trying to calm her husband down.

"Shela, I am sorry. Mom, I am sorry. Raquel, how could you?" Jermaine asked.

"Daddy, I know you have done a lot and I did not do this on purpose. I am so sorry!" Raquel stood up to plead with her father and try to get him to understand that she was sincerely sorry.

Shela stood up to call Jermaine's name because he started hollering uncontrollably.

"Raquel, I cannot believe you. You want to be a statistic? Just because you come from the projects does not mean you have to act like the projects."

"Daddy, please!"

"Jermaine!" Shela and her mother yelled, trying to get him to calm down.

"No, I am disgusted with you, Girl."

"Jermaine!" Shela and Mrs. Johnston called out.

"No!" Jermaine said as he reached out and grabbed Raquel by her shoulders and began to holler in her face and shake her.

"Dad," Raquel hollered as she cried hard. "You did this to me. You have been touching me since Mom died, and six months ago or so when you came home drunk, you raped me. Yes, you did this to me. You made me have sex with you. I was a virgin, Dad, this is what we went to counseling for, remember? Because you had molested me! I kept the rape to myself because I knew you did not know what happened because you were drunk, but then, I ended up pregnant and scared."

"Oh hell no! What did you just say, Raquel?" Shela asked with an evil, disgusted look on her face.

"Raquel, what?" Jermaine asked, and he threw up his hands as if he were reaching out to the Lord for help.

"What is really going on, Jermaine? You raped your daughter? You raped Raquel?" Shela asked.

"Shela, I thought I was your daughter too?" Raquel said as she reached over to hug Shela, with tears streaming down her face.

"Raquel, you are saying a whole lot here. I cannot register all this right now."

"Jermaine and Shela, I am going outside with my husband," Mrs. Johnston said. "You three work this mess out. I can't listen to it anymore. This is your family business, and I have no business being a part of it."

"Mom, please don't go," Shela begged.

"Shela, that is your husband and your daughter. My opinion does not matter." With that, Mrs. Johnston walked out of the house, shaking her head.

"Raquel, I am so sorry," Jermaine said. "I am sorry! There is no excuse, and I won't be making anything up. I should not have done this."

"So this is true, Jermaine," Shela asked, shaking her head as tears began to flow.

"Shela, Raquel is not a liar. My wife died tragically along with her mother and father a few years ago. I loved my wife, and I had never been with another woman and did not want another woman. I started drinking heavily every night and almost lost my job. While I was trying to get over my wife, the fact that Raquel is identical to her had me going crazy. That is no excuse, and this never should have happened. Raquel, I am so sorry. Shela, I am so sorry." Jermaine began to cry hard and beg and plea for Shela and Raquel to forgive him.

"Daddy, it is okay," Raquel cried. "We have already talked about it and gotten over it. You already repented to God, and He has forgiven you. We did counseling, remember, Daddy? I never wanted it to come up again. Shela, you are everything I need, and you promised me you would not leave me or my father."

"Raquel, I love you and your father. That was not a lie. I just need a moment right now. I can't do this. What have I gotten myself into? Is this what I asked God for? Were my prayers in vain?"

"So you didn't mean what you said?" Raquel asked. "I knew it, Shela. My life has been full of disappointments since the day I was born. It's okay. I am used to it."

Shela grabbed Raquel, and they hugged each other, tightly crying in each other's arms.

Jermaine left the house, walking down the street. He reached for his phone and called Pastor Hodges.

17

"Pastor Hodges speaking."

"Pastor Hodges, this is Jermaine again."

"Hey, Man. I see you made it back, my happily married, new armor-bearer."

"Pastor," Jermaine said, sniffling. "I really need to talk."

"Jermaine, is everything okay?"

"Pastor, please!"

"Where are you?"

"Down the street from Shela's mom's house on Fifty Second and Reddick Street."

"I'm on my way."

Pastor Hodges prayed as he drove over to pick Jermaine up. "Lord, touch and move, make a way out of no way. Not by might, nor by power, but by your spirit, said the Lord of hosts. I speak to the mountain, and I believe Jermaine will make it over. Lord, give him strength. Lord, give him peace. Lord, bless his heart. Do it, Lord, right now!"

When Pastor Hodges arrived, he told Jermaine to get in. "Let me pull down here to the Target off Seventy-Second Street. Jermaine, what is going on?"

"Pastor, I tried to talk to you about my past, and you shut me down. Now I need to talk so I can get past my past and move on to a future with my wife and daughter."

"What is it, Jermaine?"

"Pastor, my wife her mother, and father were tragically killed in a car accident while her mother was trying to rush her father to the hospital."

"Okay, Jermaine."

"Pastor, I loved my wife. She was my only love, and I never wanted another. I started drinking heavily and smoking weed everyday with Big Blue, and my life started to crumble right before my eyes. Raquel looks just like her mother, Pastor, and that is no excuse, but I molested my daughter while I was drunk. I thought my wife had come back to me.

"Jermaine, you what?"

"Pastor, I know, and I am sorry. So now I get back from my vacation, and they tell me my daughter is pregnant!"

"Raquel?"

"Pastor, I knew I touched her because we went to counseling for that. I did not know there was a time when I raped my own daughter though. What kind of a man am I?"

"Jermaine!"

"Pastor, Raquel said that this happened like six months ago. Pastor, I would never intentionally rape my daughter."

"Honestly, Jermaine, I don't know what to say. This is new for me." Pastor said, grabbing his forehead, looking very concerned.

"Pastor, you said for me to leave the past behind me."

"Jermaine, I also said you will still have consequences for your past choices and decisions."

"Pastor, I can't lose my wife!"

"How is Raquel?"

"She appears to be doing great, Pastor. We did counseling for this, but like I said, I did not know we actually had intercourse. She has already been delivered from this, and I was fine too until she told me this. I think she thought I knew. Pastor, I don't know. I am so confused right now."

"Son, you've got to pray. I have seen married couples fix their marriages over things bigger than this. Trust God, Jermaine! He can do anything."

"Pastor?"

"Jermaine!"

"Pastor, this is the last thing I would have expected to do to my child. My mother's boyfriend raped and beat me and my brothers for two years before he beat my mother to death and then shot himself. That is why we were all sent to foster care, so I know how this feels. The first time I came to your church with Shela, you were doing a series on generational curses. That was when God touched my heart regarding my childhood and about how I did what was done to me, to my own child, knowing how bad it made me feel."

"Jermaine," Pastor Hodges said, "Go get your family and go home."

"Shela is never going to go for this, Pastor and she really does not have to."

"Go get your wife and your daughter and go home." Pastor Hodges pulled up at the house and Jermaine got out. He went up to knock on the door with his eyes puffy and red.

"Come in, Jermaine," Mr. Johnston said while he and his wife stood there.

"No, Sir," Jermaine replied. "Could you have Shela and Raquel come out so we can go home please? I am so sorry, Mr. and Mr. Johnston, and I promise to fix this. I really love Shela, and I promise to be the best husband ever."

"Shela and Raquel, time to go!" Mr. Johnston said. "The man of the house has spoken."

"Dad," Shela said.

"Shela Baby, you have a husband now. Work out your differences with him. If you need me, I am here, but talk to him first."

"That's right Baby." Mrs. Johnston said. "You've got to give Jermaine a chance to speak his piece."

"Good-bye," the Johnston's said.

"Good-bye," Jermaine, Shela, and Raquel said.

The ride home was very quiet, but everyone was unable to stop crying. When they arrived home, they each went into different rooms.

18

"Lord, help me please! I truly believe Jermaine is my husband. But this I cannot handle, and I refuse to be a part of something like this. Lord, give me peace in the midst of this storm. I feel deceived, God. Lord, help me please!" Shela got down on her knees and cried aloud, unable to control herself.

"This is all my fault," Raquel said. "I knew this was all too good to be true, me with a mom again. Yeah right! What was I thinking? Shela is perfect. Lord, I really need her," Raquel screamed out loud. "I know you put us together on purpose. Lord, please work this out."

Raquel stood up, looked in the mirror, and rubbed her belly. "I never would have thought I would be having a baby by my father and not my husband, but like grandma said, everything happens for a reason."

"If I haven't learned anything else from Pastor Hodges, I learned that a family that prays together stays together," Jermaine said with a lot of power and authority in his voice.

He raised his right fist to show he was serious. "Raquel and Shela, come in here please!"

Shela peeked out her door, looking down on the ground. "Yes, Jermaine."

"Yes, Daddy?" Raquel asked.

"Can you both please come in here? There are some things I need to say and do right now." Shela and Raquel both walked to the spare bedroom where Jermaine was standing and turned to him to see what it was, he had to say.

"Raquel, Baby, I love you so much, and I am truly sorry for what I have done." Jermaine reached out to rub Raquel's shoulder.

"And Shela, My Love," he said while grabbing both of Shela's hands, as she continued to look down and avoided his eyes. "I am sincerely sorry for taking you through this experience. I want to be with you for the rest of my life. All this happened before I even knew you, and Baby, that is no excuse, but I pray we can work through this mess and be a happy family."

"Let's grab hands, and I am going to pray for God's blessing over this household. In the precious name of Jesus, Lord, I thank and praise you, and I believe you, for restoration and reconciliation in this household right now. Lord, I truly and sincerely come to you as boldly as I know how, asking that you would forgive me for everything I have done that is displeasing in your sight or against the knowledge of your word. Lord, bless my heart, my mind, and my soul. Lord, mend our broken hearts and heal this family. Touch Raquel and move in her so mightily, God. Make her a vessel full of your blessings. Touch Shela and allow your will to be done in her and through her. Encourage each one of us, heal us, destroy every yoke in us, bless us, change us, and show yourself strong in us. Lord, do the impossible! Lord, perform the incredible! I trust you, God, and I am truly persuaded you can and will perform your word, right now. I believe you, God, in Jesus's most holy name, Amen."

"Shela, I really want to talk to you," Jermaine said, facing Shela with his arms extended for a hug. "When you are ready, please let me know. I promise I did not lift your spirits just to let you down. I married you for love, but I do have a past. I'll tell you everything you want to know Shela, but please don't leave me. Please be my wife. I promise to love you forever, and I promise our future will be great."

∞∞∞∞∞∞

Hurting and upset, Shela walked away to her room and laid on her bed. After lying there thinking for about an hour, she picked up the house phone to call her mother.

"Hello, Mom."

"Hey, Shela. How are you doing?"

"Mom! How am I? I'm terrible! My husband, my baby's father, is having a baby by his biological daughter. Who does that, Mom?"

"Shela, I know you did not know this, but Raquel is about six months pregnant now. You have known Jermaine for like five months right? This happened before you started dating."

"Mom, I am almost five months pregnant."

"Okay, Shela! First of all, you slept with him pretty quickly, and you really did not get to know him very well! Did you ever question his past? Come on now, let's be real."

"No, I did not, but—"

"But what, Shela? Do you not have a past?" Her mother said, quickly cutting her off with much attitude.

"What? Mom, are you kidding me? You can't be serious?"

"Shela, the question is, do you have a past? Are there things you have done that no one knows about and that you regret?"

"Mom! Are you defending Jermaine's behavior?"

"Evangelist Shela, I am keeping it one hundred percent real. Jermaine's behavior is dead wrong. What he has done is sick, and it proclaims him to be a pedophile. Rape is worthy of jail time and maybe charges should be pressed, but he is not just Jermaine anymore, he is your husband. This is the man you said you love! Shela, vows are sacred! This is the man you have vowed to support until death do you part! Do you think my marriage has been perfect? Do you think I've always wanted to stay? Well, love kept me here. My husband is human and imperfect just like me, and he gave me a marriage I believe is worth fighting for. Although it has not been easy, this has been the best thirty-six years of my life. You prayed for this, and I believe God gave you his best. The best has flaws too! Do you love him?"

Shela sat there on the phone in disbelief. This was not what she wanted her mother to say. She was ready to man bash, and she was looking for a way out. She did not reply to her mother, but she sat shaking her head, wondering when she was going to awaken from her nightmare.

"Shela!" her mother demanded, "Do you love him? Do not sit there ignoring me!"

"Mom, you know I do." Shela fell back on her bed with her left hand on her forehead.

"Do you believe your new marriage is worth fighting for? Can you take the good with the bad? What do you think?"

"Mom, you know I do." *Is this really happening?* Shela thought.

"Well, get up, wipe your face, and just like you are talking to me, go talk to your husband."

"I can't right now, Mom."

"Well, I am hanging up and do not call me back until you have talked to your husband. I love you, Shela." Immediately, Shela's mother hung up the phone.

"Mom! I cannot believe she hung up the phone. Is she really serious? And then she had the nerve to pull the Evangelist card. Wow! God, if I never needed you before, I surely need you now. I mean, I do love him." Shela put her phone on the charger and started to count on her fingers the great things about Jermaine. "I just had the perfect cruise with him. He has treated me like royalty since day one. Lord, what am I supposed to do? I really need to hear from you now."

∞∞∞∞∞∞

Ring, ring.

"Who is this calling me?" Shela grabbed her cell phone from her purse. "First Lady? Hello, First Lady."

"Shela?"

"Yes, Ma'am."

"Shela, Jermaine met with Pastor this afternoon. I am so sorry!"

"First Lady"—Shela began to cry again—"How can something so perfect turn out to be so tragic?"

"Shela," First Lady said very graciously, "I am going to tell you this: God works in mysterious ways. You will never know why God moves the way he moves but know that everything he does has a good reason. Pastor and I have had our ups and downs, but as his wife, I vowed to support him. I am not saying be stupid, but anything that happened before you came into the picture is the past, and Jermaine's past does not determine his future. Wasn't it you who spoke that message at our singles conference: 'Your Past Has No Relevance In Your Future.' Huh, Evangelist Shela Riley? Won't God try you in the very message you preach?"

"Yes, Ma'am. That was me," Shela said, disappointed again because no one was trying to tell her to get out immediately.

"Well, Shela, I truly believe God is testing your faith."

"First Lady, I just prayed, and I believe God sent your call for a confirmation of what my mother just said. Thanks a lot."

"You are welcome, Shela. Be strong and depend on the Lord for all your decisions right now. It was Him who said, 'Cast all your cares on me because I care for you,' right?"

Shela got off the phone and went to run herself some bathwater in her Roman tub. She turned on the bubbles, lit some candles, turned on her CeCe Winans CD, turned out the lights, got in the tub, and laid back to relax on her bath pillow.

She had to help herself relieve some stress, and this was how she always did it.

Jermaine walked into Raquel's room to apologize to her again. He felt really bad for what he had done, and he could not stop everything from playing in his head over and over again. He knew the one thing Raquel had desired since her mother died was a woman to come in, mother her, and marry her father. He knew in his heart that Shela was the one to make both of their dreams come true, and he also knew he had totally messed that up.

"Dad, I believe God is going to work this out for us, 'ye of little faith,'" Raquel said, quoting the word of God. "I have seen God move in some crazy ways, Dad, since I learned exactly who He is."

"Raquel, I hear you, but—"

"But what, Daddy? Let God move! Leave it alone, Dad! Get your hands out of it!" Raquel chuckled.

"Okay, Baby. You are right. That really touched me. I mean, I really felt that. Thanks a lot. I am leaving it alone."

19

"Jermaine," Shela said, walking into the room where he was sitting with his face in his hands and elbows in his thighs; he was thinking hard.

"Yes, Shela." Jermaine stood up. He had not expected her to ever come in but was happy she did.

"Jermaine, I love you with all my heart. I meant my vows. I was not just reciting them. I have always dreamed of having a husband like you. You are truly a good man. Right now, my mind has a million different thoughts going on. I am trying to focus, but I cannot. Jermaine, I am so hurt, mad, and embarrassed, but I am more in love with you. I want to be with you for the rest of my life, but we have really got to talk."

"Okay, Shela. I will talk about anything, but please don't leave me and Raquel."

"Jermaine, you raped your daughter and have been molesting her for a while."

"'Molested, not have been molesting. It is past tense."

"I don't know why I am just now asking questions. I guess I was so excited to finally have a man that I avoided the important things. Why did you rape your daughter?"

"Shela, let me be perfectly honest. I am not making any excuses or anything, but I believe it has something to do with the whole 'generational curse' thing. That is something I never even heard of until I came to the church and Pastor Hodges was preaching that series."

"Generational curse? Okay, what are you saying?"

"Well, Shela, this is so embarrassing, but let me begin here. When I was younger, my mother's boyfriend, molested me and my brothers on a regular basis. I thought it was only me until one day I came home from school and walked in on him and my youngest brother. After talking to my other brothers, we all thought we were the only one, and we were too embarrassed to say anything. After I witnessed him doing that to my brother and we all talked, we went to tell my mother. She cursed him out, put him out, and called the police to press charges. Well, the next day when we got home from school, our mother was lying on the floor in the kitchen beat to death, and there was her boyfriend, dead beside her with a bullet in his head and the gun still hanging on to his pointer finger."

"Jermaine, I am so sorry to hear that. You never told me that. All you said to me was that you lost your mother as a kid. I thought maybe she had some disease or something."

"Well, Shela, I have never discussed it with anyone. No one ever asked, and I never wanted to burden anyone with my mess."

"Jermaine, that was important information to share with someone. You held that for all these years?"

"Shela, where I come from no one asks questions and you don't speak until you are spoken to. I have lived in several foster homes, with and without my brothers, and the abuse, whether it was verbal, sexual, emotional, physical, or mental, never stopped. I was declared the bad kid no matter where I was, and no one ever wanted to hear what I had to say. I was the liar, they said, so no one paid me any attention. That is why I never shared my story. Why share if no one believes you and you end up being the one in trouble anyways?"

"I am so sorry, Jermaine."

"It is okay. When I turned sixteen, I got a job at the convenient store up the street from the foster home I was placed in, and that is where I met Dakar, a.k.a. D-Nice. He was the cleanest, realest street hustler, and I joined his team. He moved me out of where I was and in with him and his wife. They helped me to make money and save money all at the same time. My wife and I were high school sweethearts. At eighteen, I married her and made the decision to leave my old life in St. Louis and start over in Omaha, Nebraska, where I could be happy. D-Nice gave me a nice piece of change, a nice car, and sent me on my way. I never imagined I would be doing the very thing that messed me up and almost caused me to commit suicide, to my own daughter. When Rachel died, I became a drunk. That was what I learned takes your problems away. Boy, was that a lie! It makes you forget what you did, but it magnifies your problem in the process. I could not stop drinking, and I looked at my daughter as my wife. I have met and dated several women, but none of those women were near what I knew I was searching for. I wanted nothing from them and then you came along."

"I am so sorry, Jermaine. I guess I never inquired about your life. I was so excited about having you that I never cared about your past."

"Shela."

"Not that I didn't care. But, Jermaine, your past is your past. As long as you are delivered, who am I to judge? I am not God. What you did to your daughter is in any of us, but God chose to allow it to happen in your life, for whatever reason or another."

"Shela, thank you so much for saying that. My life has been pretty screwed up until the day I met you, and you turned me on to God. Knowing God has been the foundation of the new me. Shela, you have lived the perfect life, and although I am not perfect, I am a really good man! I promise to only get better. Pastor Hodges is the first man who has ever acted like a father to me. He's the only man to ever encourage me, and I am over forty. I never knew life like this and never imagined knowing it."

"Jermaine, I am far from perfect."

"Right, Shela," Jermaine replied, because he knew Shela always had it going on.

"Jermaine, let me share some things with you. I never tried to lie to you, but you really never asked. First of all, you know I am a prosecutor, right?"

"Of course, Shela, and a soon-to-be judge."

"Well, baby, I give maximum punishment to any sex offender who is found guilty."

"There is nothing wrong with that. I guess that's what I would be considered, and I need to be thrown in jail."

"Jermaine, I did not say that to condemn you. Let me tell you what causes me to do that. When I was twenty-one years old, I met this guy who appeared to be very nice. He was a college student just like me. We dated for about five months, and our relationship was nice. One day, he invited me over to hang out with him and some friends, and I accepted the invitation. Anyways, I went over there, and no one else ever showed up. He kept looking out, acting like he was wondering where everyone was too. Since no one ever came, we watched a couple of movies and played a couple of games. After a while, although I was having fun, I was ready to go home. That jerk refused to let me leave. He tore all my clothes off and forced me to have sex with him. He raped me. Jermaine, I wanted to be a virgin when I married my husband, and he robbed me of that."

"He did, Honey, but I thought you were a virgin."

"No, and not only that, he got me pregnant."

"What?"

"I had an abortion, Jermaine, and this is the first time in my life I have ever talked openly about it. No one knows about the rape or the baby. I have never been comfortable enough to share that story with anyone."

"Shela, I am so sorry."

"Originally, I went to school only to be lawyer because I believe I can debate well, but after my rape incident, I wanted to be able to punish everyone for what my attacker did to me. So, I continued on to be a prosecutor."

"Wow, I am so sorry. I love you, Shela!"

"I know you do, Jermaine, but when I heard Raquel say you raped her, it took me back to when I was twenty-one years old and a victim of rape myself."

"I understand that, and I am truly sorry. What can I do? I want to be with you, please!"

"I want to be with you too, Jermaine."

"So can you forgive me? What must I do to win your forgiveness?"

"I do forgive you, Jermaine, and if fifteen-year-old Raquel can forgive you, I guess I need to forgive my attacker. Let's go talk to Raquel."

"Okay, Babe." Jermaine and Shela walked into the room with Raquel to talk about everything.

"Raquel, we are sorry for all of the confusion earlier," Jermaine said.

"Raquel, I love you, and I vowed to be with you for the rest of your life and to be your mother, and I am going to be here. I can get past the past, and I promise to never bring it up again."

"Wow, Shela! Are you serious?"

"Yes, I am."

"See, Daddy? I knew she was the one for us."

20

"This is Elaine Tucker."

"Hello, Counselor Elaine T. This is Raquel."

"Raquel, we have not seen or heard from you in two and a half months."

"I know. I am so sorry. I have had a lot going on these last two and a half months, that's why."

"Well, you know my first question, don't you?"

"What?"

"Have you seen the doctor? The last time I saw you, you had not seen one. And have you been taking your prenatal pills?"

"I have been taking my pills, and yes, I have been going to the doctor. My dad did have insurance, thank God."

"So you talked to your dad?"

"Yes, Ma'am."

"Wow! How did he take the news?"

"Honestly, Counselor Elaine T., he was very upset and was going to kill me, I think."

"Really? Well, thank God you are still here." Counselor Elaine T. chuckled a little.

"I know." Raquel laughed out loud.

"So what stopped him from killing you?"

"His new wife and my grandmother."

"He's married now?"

"Yes, happily."

"Wow!"

"Not only that, Counselor Elaine T., my new mother is having a baby too."

"Wow, again! Are you serious?"

"Yes, Ma'am."

"You know, Raquel, I came by your house a couple of times to talk to you and your dad."

"You did? Why?"

"Because Denna reported that you were raped and I had to do a follow-up."

"But I told you I was not raped."

"You did tell me that, and I put it in my report. But I wanted to make sure I was doing my job, so I decided to check after you one more time."

"Really? Well, we moved." Raquel had a little attitude in her voice.

"You did?"

"Yes, we live out west now with my new mother. My whole life has changed for the better."

"Raquel, I am so happy for you. You are a very strong-willed, determined, young woman, and I expect great things from you."

"Thanks, Counselor Elaine T. I really appreciate that."

"So how does your baby's daddy feel?"

"What?"

"Your baby's daddy, how is he taking it? You have told him, haven't you?"

"You know, that young man died."

"He died?"

"Yes, Ma'am, he is dead. God has a way of doing things that are definitely not our way."

"He's dead?" Counselor Elaine T. asked again.

"Dead!"

"I'm so sorry to hear that. You are taking that quite well."

"It's okay. When God moves, we rejoice, and this was definitely a move of God."

"How long ago was this?"

"This happened months ago."

"Well, you didn't share this information the first time I saw you."

"God had to show me what to say and how to say it."

"What?"

Raquel chuckled a little at her answer and repeated, "God had to show me what to say and how to say it."

"Okay, I guess it is not for me to understand."

"Counselor Elaine T., thank you for everything. Can I speak to Ms. Denna?"

"Let me get her for you." She put Raquel on hold and called for Ms. Denna to pick up line one.

"This is Denna."

"Ms. Denna, hello. This is Raquel."

"Hey, Sweetie! Where have you been? How are you doing? I have been praying for you."

"I knew someone was praying. I have been home with my family, and I am doing very well."

"You sound great, girl. I knew God was going to favor you, Raquel. He has a way of working things out. Are you seeing a doctor?"

"Yes, Ma'am."

"Great! You take care of that baby, and if you ever need anything from me, I want you to call me on my cell phone. You got a pen or pencil and paper?"

"Yes, I'm ready."

Denna gave Raquel her number.

"I got it and thank you so much again. Ms. Denna, you were the first person to speak life into my dead situation. You encouraged me when you could have talked about me like a dog. You prayed for me. I mean, you touched my heart in so many ways, and you gave me hope. That is what has helped me to keep my head up."

"Wow, Raquel, Honey, thanks a lot. I needed to hear that. I give God all the glory. I try my best, and I am thankful that you shared that with me. None of us are here to judge. We are all here to help one another. You just made my day."

"Glad I could do something for you, but it will never repay you for what you have done for me."

"Raquel, it has been wonderful talking to you. Thank you so much for calling me, but I have to get back to my patients. You have the number. Use it, Sweetie."

"I will. Good-bye."

"Good-bye."

21

"Hello."

"Hey, Delila."

"Raquel! Oh my God! I can't believe you! Where have you been?"

"I am so sorry, Delila. I have had so much going on these last couple months, and I just could not talk about it."

"I understand, but my main concern is, are you okay?"

"I am wonderful. Actually, I have never been better. My life has totally turned around for the better."

"Raquel, you have never sounded like this before, and I mean never. You really sound good, Girl."

"I do? Well, I am serious. I have never known that life could be this great."

"Fill me in. Did you win the lottery or something?"

"Not exactly, but close to it."

"Wow, Raquel!"

"Delila, can you call Martine please?"

"Okay, hold on."

"Hello."

"Hey, Martine," Delila and Raquel said.

"Raquel, is that you?" Martine said full of joy.

"Yes, it is!"

"Girl, how are you? You just disappeared from the face of the earth."

"I am great, Girl. Better than ever."

"It sounds like it."

"So fill us in on life," Delila said.

"Well, first of all, my dad and Shela are married.

"They got married?" Martine said surprised.

"Yes, they did, and they are truly happy."

"Wow, that was fast," Delila said.

"It was, but true love has its own way of doing things. And we moved with Shela."

"Well, I knew you moved," said Martine. "I was wondering what happened."

"I thought your dad was trying to get you away from the hood because of your new baby," Delila replied.

"No, Girl. Shela has a big house, remember? It was better for us to go that route. I mean, she owns her house, and we just rented. We didn't have our stuff moved in until they were gone on their honeymoon."

"Wow," said Martine.

"And get this, Shela is pregnant," Raquel exclaimed with a big smile on her face.

"Wow! She is?" Delila cupped her mouth with her left hand.

"Really?" Martine chimed in.

"She is."

"How far is she?" Delila asked.

"Six and a half months."

"A little over a month under you?" Delila asked again.

"Yes."

"Wow," Martine and Delila said.

"But Shela is very happy and excited, and so am I. She and my dad are going to help me raise my baby."

"I figured that," replied Delila.

"It's going to be almost like twins, just like me and Marshon," Martine replied, happy as a lark.

"I know right," said Delila.

"Shela is having a bouncing baby boy."

"Wow! A boy and a girl." Martine was thinking, *this is just like me and Marshon.*

"Well, my daddy's son is going to be named Jermaine Jr., and my baby girl's name is going to be Shermaine."

"Shermaine?" Martine inquired.

"Yes. That is Shela and Jermaine put together."

"Beautiful," said Martine.

"That is pretty cute," Delila said.

"Girl, my dad thought of it. That was going to be the name of their baby if it was a girl."

"What about your baby's daddy?" Delila asked.

"Y'all, he died."

"He died? Oh my God, Raquel!" Martine questioned.

"It's okay, y'all. God has a way of working things out for our good."

"Raquel, you sure are positive about this," Delila screeched.

"Delila, wasn't it you who told me we could focus on the negative but where would that get us? God has been good to me, y'all. I went from public housing to a four-bedroom, three-and-a-half-bathroom house, from no mother to a wonderful mother, from a daddy to a saved daddy, and now I am blessed to have a baby of my own."

"You are right, Raquel," Delila said. "I know that. Thanks for reminding me. It is great to see you recognizing the goodness of the Lord."

"It took me a minute, but now I realize the things of God are only revealed to his own, and I am his own."

"Wow," Martine said.

"'Wow is right," said Delila. "Sounds like you've been doing a lot of churchin' too."

"I have. And I would not change it for the world. Well, y'all, I have got to go eat and go to bed. I love y'all."

"We love you too."

"Stay in touch and please don't go another almost three months before you call. Oh and I want to be at the hospital with you," Delila said.

"Me too," Martine chimed in.

"I won't do that again, I promise. And I will definitely let you both know when I go to the hospital. Alright, good-bye."

"Good-bye."

22

PLEASE JOIN US
FOR A BABY SHOWER!

Date: Saturday January 22nd

Time: 1:30 PM - 4:00 PM

At: Intentional Deliverance Nondenominational Church
2578 Pratt St.
Omaha, NE 68111

Registered at: TARGET AND WALMART

RSVP by January 3rd to First Lady Alma Ruth Hodges at 402-451-1821

First Lady Hodges, Mrs. Johnston, and a few of First Lady Hodges's armor-bearers got together to plan a double baby shower for Shela and Raquel. Each gave their personal list of invitees, which added up to about one hundred people. On top of that, the entire church was invited.

Shela was a very well-liked woman by many, so the fellowship hall was full of church friends, rich executives, and top city officials. Raquel had many old and new classmates that showed up as well as friends from her old neighborhood. Many of the people from Jermaine's work also attended.

There were tables full of gifts and cards and a fellowship hall full of over two hundred people. The gifts included two gift certificates for two years' worth of pampers and wipes, two beds, two car seat strollers, several diaper bags, bottles, bags full of clothes, and more pampers.

23

"Shela, are you sure you want to do this?" Jermaine asked, making sure his wife was up for the task.

"Jermaine, whether I want to or not, I need to do this."

"You need to do it? Baby, I am just making sure."

"I am one hundred percent sure."

"Okay, then. Come on. I got your back, Shela."

"Thank you so much, Honey. I love you so much. Please hug me before we go."

"Of course, Baby." Jermaine reached over to hug his beautiful wife and kiss her lightly on the lips as the elevator doors opened.

"The fifteenth floor?" Jermaine asked when he saw Shela push the button. "Are you kidding me?"

"No, Honey, the fifteenth floor." They both chuckled. The elevator doors opened, and they walked down the hall to room 1509.

"Good morning, Shela. Is this your new husband? How are you?"

"Hello, Imery. I am great, and yes, this is my husband, Jermaine. Honey, this is Imery, the Executive Assistant. Is Douglas available?"

"Douglas? Of course he is, Shela."

"Imery, please let Douglas know I would like to see him. It is very important."

"Judge McCarthy, Shela is here to see you."

"Shela?" Judge McCarthy asked. "Shela Johnston?"

"Yes, Sir. Shela Johnston."

"No, Shela Riley!" Jermaine answered.

"Shela Riley, Sir."

"Please send her in."

"Shela, would you like for me to stay here while you do this?"

"Jermaine, please."

"I want you to be comfortable."

"I am just fine, Honey. You seem like the one who's uncomfortable." Shela laughed a little.

"Okay, Baby." Jermaine smiled, grabbed Shela's hand, and they walked to the back together. Jermaine opened the door, and they walked in.

"Shela!" Judge McCarthy stood up to greet her and Jermaine with a handshake.

"Hello, Douglas."

"And you must be the new mister."

"Yes, Sir. Jermaine Riley."

"Jermaine, what an honor. So Shela, what brings you to my chambers this fine morning?"

"Douglas, um..." Shela turned away, embarrassed.

"Shela, go ahead," Jermaine said.

"Douglas, we really have some unfinished business."

"Unfinished business?"

"Yes, Douglas. Twenty-one years ago, we dated, and I believed we were friends. I trusted you, and you raped me."

"Shela! For the last fifteen years, I have tried to talk to you about that night, and you have shut me down each time. I know what I did was wrong. I am truly sorry for taking the one thing from you that you can never get back. I stole your virginity. Jermaine, your wife is a jewel. She has been perfect since the day I met her twenty-one years ago. She is classy, laid-back, and full of love. I allowed my flesh to get the best of me, and yes, I raped Shela Renee Johnston. I am not proud at all. I was totally wrong for my actions, and I can never give back what I took. But I promise you, I am sorry from the bottom of my heart. Shela, I will tell the world. I would apologize in front of the media. I will do whatever it takes to get you to forgive me and release me of this act I committed."

"I just want to know why."

"Shela, I fell in love with you, and I really wanted you. I had a few drinks, and honestly, I did not know how to take no for an answer. I thought you loved me and wanted me too. I could not control myself. Again, I am so sorry. Is there anything I can do?"

"Douglas, for the last twenty-one years, I never realized how much hatred and bitterness I have had bottled up inside of me or why it was there. Because of my attack, I have no sympathy for any sex offenders. I was pregnant with your child, and I killed our child because I was hurt, embarrassed, and discouraged."

"You were pregnant?"

"Yes, for about three weeks."

"Shela! Wow! I wish I would have known. A couple of years after that incident I had a minor surgery. My wife and I tried for years to have a baby, and we found out later I was sterile and unable to produce due to that minor surgery. I can't believe this."

"I am sorry to hear that, Douglas."

"So, Shela, can this be the beginning of a new relationship between us? When I got saved, that one moment in time tore me up. And I promise, I repented and gave it to God. That is why I was trying to talk to you. I needed to make sure I was totally forgiven, and until now, I never really felt that release."

"Douglas, I sincerely forgive you, and I apologize for holding on to this for so long. I believe God is going to be able to do some things in both our lives because of this moment right here."

"Thank you so much, Shela. Jermaine, thank you so much for supporting your wife and taking time out to come here and help us to complete this moment."

"Thank you too, Douglas, and I promise to never bring it up again."

"You are welcome, Man. There are things in all our lives we need to give to God so he can make our outcome great."

24

"Yes, Raquel, they are five minutes apart," Shela said.

"Well, let's go. By the time we get to the hospital, our new baby is going to be popping out," Jermaine said excitedly.

"Daddy!" Raquel chuckled, and they all laughed.

Raquel had already packed her hospital bag a week ago. She had become overly excited about her new baby girl's arrival into the world. She called Delila and Martine to let them know she was on her way to the hospital so they could meet here there.

Jermaine had learned how to deal with attitudes, walking around the house with two pregnant ladies. He found himself working harder than ever, trying to make them happy and to cater to their every need.

Shela had enjoyed her pregnancy so much. She took the morning sickness with a smile. Every cramp and stomachache made her more anxious for her baby to arrive. Shela called her parents to let them know Raquel was on her way to the hospital so they could meet her there.

Jermaine, Shela, and Raquel got in the car and made their way to Bergan Mercy Hospital Birthing Center Triage. This was the most beautiful, state-of-the-art women's hospital ever made, and it was located in Omaha, Nebraska. The hospital was considered a historical landmark, and people flew in from all over the world to give birth in it. As Jermaine pulled up to the glass front for valet parking, the attendant rushed right over to give first-class service.

∞∞∞∞∞∞

"Good evening. May I have your name please."

"Raquel Riley."

"Dr. Malaika Robbins was supposed to call in for us, and she said the room would be ready," Shela replied.

"Okay. Let me call the charge nurse real quick for you. Hello, Nurse Enchantria, did Dr. Malaika call in a patient?"

"Yes! We are waiting on Raquel Riley."

"She just arrived."

"Okay, send her to room eighteen."

"You got it. Alright, you guys can go back through that door on the left to room eighteen, which will be the fourth room on the right.

"Thank you so much," they all said as they walked to the back.

"Hello, everyone," Nurse Dancer said as she stepped into the room. "Who is Raquel? I see two basketballs."

"I am."

"Alright. I want you to change into this gown. I am going to come back, check your vital signs, and get you hooked up to this baby heart monitor and this contraction monitor. And then I'm going to check and see how far you have dilated."

"Okay."

As Nurse Dancer walked out, a young man with a nice business suit walked in, holding a clipboard full of paperwork.

"Hello, everyone. I am Xayden, your Financial Counselor. I am here to get your insurance card, a valid piece of identification, and your co-pay."

"Let me get all of that for you. It's in my wallet." Jermaine reached inside his wallet to give him everything he had just requested. He already knew there was no co-pay for Raquel's actual delivery so he let Xayden know that as he handed over his identification and Raquel's insurance card.

"I'll be right back to return these things after I make copies."

"Okay, Sir." Jermaine and Shela left the room so they could give Raquel her privacy as she undressed.

"Baby," Shela said. "I am feeling a little woozy. I really need to have a seat."

"Let's see if Raquel is finished. You can just have a seat in there!" Jermaine said. "You need me to get you a nurse?"

"No, Jermaine. I think I will be alright, but I definitely need to have a seat. Let's knock on the door. I feel myself getting a headache, and I am starting to feel all warm."

"It's probably this hospital getting you all worked up, Love."

"You are probably right."

They knocked on the door. Raquel was all done and lying in the bed, so they went in. Shela had a seat while Jermaine massaged her shoulders.

Xayden walked back in the room to return their identification and insurance cards, and then walked back out thanking them for everything.

"How are you feeling, Raquel?" Jermaine asked.

"I am just ready, Dad. I am so tired of being pregnant, and these pains are hurting me so bad."

"I know the feeling of being ready, Raquel," Shela said, rubbing her stomach and looking distressed.

"Are you okay, Mom?" Raquel asked as another sharp pain ran through her belly and caused her to scream.

"Yes, Baby. I am alright, I think."

"Okay, I am back." Nurse Dancer got Raquel all hooked up to the monitors, checked her vital signs, then checked to see how far she was dilated. "Raquel, you are five centimeters. I will be right back with your IV. I am going to go and call Dr. Malaika to see where she wants us to go from here."

"Jermaine, I think I need to lie down. I'm getting dizzy," Shela said.

"Baby, what is going on?" Jermaine asked.

"Mom, are you okay?" Raquel asked through another one of her ridiculous labor pains. "I am calling the nurse." Raquel hit the nurse call button so she could get someone in there as soon as possible.

"Sorry, Raquel," Nurse Dancer said as she walked back in the room. "I know your pains are hurting you, and I was trying to get back as quickly as possible."

"No, Nurse Dancer. It is my mom."

"My wife is not feeling well," Jermaine said, with his hands in the air and a worried look on his face.

"How far along are you, guys?" Nurse Dancer asked, while finishing the process of hooking up Raquel's IV.

"We are almost eight months, Ma'am," Jermaine answered. "Can you please call Dr. Malaika?"

"Sir, let me go and see if we have any rooms free."

"Call Dr. Malaika," Shela said. "She'll make a room free. She's got clout in this hospital."

Nurse Dancer came back into the room with Nurse Enchantria so that she could finish working with Raquel, and Shela and Jermaine could be taken care of. "We are going to be taking you two to room 7 right down the hall, so we can check your vital signs, and see what is going on with you."

While Nurse Dancer and Nurse Enchantria were trying to explain what was going on, Delila and Martine walked through the door. This put a bright smile on Raquel's face because she did not want her dad to have to choose who to stay with and who to leave alone. Now that her friends were there, her dad could go and be with his wife and be comfortable that Raquel was safe and happy.

"Hey, Raquel," Delila and Martine said. They were so happy to be at the hospital with their friend and proud that they would be able to see her baby being born.

"Hello, guys." Raquel squeezed her eyes together hard and balled up her fists so that she could endure the pain of the contraction that was hurting her.

"Raquel, are you going to be okay?" Martine asked.

120

"I will be fine. I am ready though. This hurts so bad."

"Okay, Raquel. I am going to need for you to lean over to your left side and be as still as possible. Dr. Malaika ordered an epidural. This will take your pain away in just a few minutes, but you cannot move."

"Okay." Raquel was very still as Nurse Dancer stuck the needle in her back to complete her epidural. Within fifteen minutes, Raquel was unable to feel any pain; but by the look of the monitor, you could tell her contractions were very big.

∞∞∞∞∞∞

"Mrs. Riley, your blood pressure is extremely high. Dr. Malaika is on her way. I am going to hook up this IV, so we can get some fluids going in you to help you feel a little better. Also, I am going to hook up this contraction monitor as well as the baby's heart monitor."

"Can you tell me how my daughter, Raquel, is doing please?"

"Oh, Mr. Riley, she is doing great. We just gave her an epidural so she can no longer feel any contractions. When we get ready to move her upstairs, we will be sure to let you know."

"Jermaine, I am so sorry. We are here for our daughter, and here I am laid up in pain. Hopefully this won't last long."

"Baby, you can't help that. Why are you apologizing? You just lay back and relax." Jermaine kissed Shela on her forehead and held her hand to comfort her.

∞∞∞∞∞∞

"Hey, Raquel, Sweetie, how are you feeling?" Mrs. Johnston said as she and her husband walked through the door.

"Grandma and Grandpa!" Raquel shouted happily. "I am so glad you are here. I am doing good. I'm so ready to have my baby, but I am doing good. These are my friends, Martine and Delila."

"Hello, ladies," Mr. and Mrs. Johnston said.

"Hello," Martine and Delila replied.

"Where are your parents at?" Mrs. Johnston asked.

"Mom got sick, so they took her to a room so she could rest a bit. They are in room seven."

"What? I had no idea!" Mrs. Johnston exclaimed.

"You guys can go down there. I won't feel bad. I want to know when they will be back anyways."

Mr. and Mrs. Johnston made their way down the hallway as Nurse Dancer and Nurse Enchantria came back in to check Raquel.

"Raquel, you will be glad to know you have dilated to nine centimeters, and we are on our way upstairs."

"I have?" Raquel asked, with a big smile on her face.

"Yes, Ma'am, and Dr. Malaika is in the building. Let me give her a call." Nurse Enchantria got on her phone to call Dr. Malaika and let her know Raquel was on her way upstairs.

"Oh my God, this is so exciting," Martine said. "You are really about to have your baby."

"I know, but my mom and dad aren't even in here. Nurse, can you please let them know?"

"I certainly will."

∞∞∞∞∞∞

Mr. and Mrs. Johnston were in the room visiting with Shela and Jermaine for a little while when the doctor walked in.

"Shela," Dr. Malaika said. "You have preeclampsia. Your blood pressure is too high."

"Preeclampsia?" Jermaine and Shela asked.

"Preeclampsia is a complication during pregnancy, and it affects about four or five percent of all women. It is high blood pressure and damage to the linings of the blood vessels of the brain, liver, lungs, and kidneys. There are times when it causes organ failure, convulsions, coma, and death. We are going to have to deliver your baby now.

"What about Raquel?" Jermaine asked.

"Well, you will be happy to know Raquel is on her way upstairs as we speak, ready to deliver. I am going to need for you to roll over on your left side and be perfectly still so I can administer this epidural."

Shela did exactly as she was asked, and her epidural went smoothly. Immediately after that, Shela was rushed upstairs for an emergency C-section.

25

What a joy to Jermaine, Shela, and Raquel that they had two beautiful, healthy babies.

"Lord, I thank you for this awesome blessing," Jermaine said, with his right hand raised as he looked up to the ceiling.

"Praise him, Daddy. I am thankful too. I love my baby. Look at her. She is so pretty. She's got her big brown eyes wide open starring right at me. I love you, Shermaine Marie," Raquel said as she kissed her new baby on her pretty little lips.

"I, too, am thankful," Shela said. "God sure knows how to turn a negative situation into a true blessing. A baby boy! I have always wanted a baby. Now I've got three babies and a wonderful husband. I am so satisfied, Lord."

∞∞∞∞∞∞

Four days later

"Good morning, everyone," Dr. Malaika said as she walked through the door. "How is my fine family today?"

"We are great, Doctor," Jermaine said.

"Absolutely wonderful!" Raquel exclaimed.

"Dr. Malaika, although I just had a baby, I have never felt better. I really appreciate your moving us over to this presidential family suite and giving us first-class service," Shela said.

"Girl, you've got first-class insurance," Dr. Malaika said, and they all chuckled. "No, but what did you expect for me to do for my good friend? You deserve it, Shela. Congratulations to you all!"

"Yeah, thanks a lot!" Jermaine said.

"I never would have expected this type of treatment," Raquel said. "I feel like a princess."

"You are a princess," Jermaine, Shela, and Dr. Malaika said, which made Raquel smile from ear to ear.

"You guys have a few more papers to sign, and I will officially release you."

"Okay thanks," they all responded. Dr. Malaika walked out of the room, and a studious young professional entered the room.

"Good morning, ladies and gentleman. I am Quyona. I am here to get the birth certificates signed and to take care of your social security cards for you."

"Okay, that sounds great." Jermaine said, looking over at Raquel and Shela with a smile.

"I will do you first, Ma'am," Quyona said, as she pushed up her wire-framed glasses.

"That is fine," said Shela.

"I want you to look at this paperwork and make sure we have everything correct."

"Yes, everything is fine," Shela said, after she quickly scanned the birth certificate.

"I am the father."

"Yes, Sir. I'll have a place for you to sign in just a minute." Both Jermaine and Shela signed the birth certificate, and Shela signed the social security card application.

"Okay. Now on to you, young lady," Quyona said.

"Yes, I am Raquel."

"Is the father going to sign the birth certificate?" Quyona asked.

"Well, my baby's father died. But me and my mother and father have talked about it, and I would like for my daddy to sign my baby's birth certificate."

"Yes, Quyona, I will be raising baby Shermaine!" Jermaine replied. "She is mine, and I will be signing her birth certificate."

"Raquel, I am so sorry to hear about your baby's father, but this is a first. I commend you Mr. Riley for stepping up and raising baby Shermaine. Wow!"

Raquel and Jermaine signed the birth certificate, and Raquel signed the social security card application.

"Thank you guys very much. It was so nice to meet you. Have a wonderful life." Quyona said.

"Thanks, and may you be blessed," Shela replied.

"Thanks a lot," Jermaine said.

"Ditto," Raquel said.

About thirty minutes later, Dr. Malaika returned. "Yes, I am back, and you are officially released. I will see you guys in two weeks for Jermaine IV's and Shermaine's appointments. May you guys be blessed, and if you need me, you definitely know how to get in touch with me."

"We really appreciate you and thank you once again for all you have done!" Jermaine said.

"Malaika, I love you girl, and I will give you a call next week. Thanks again!" Shela said as she hugged her good friend.

"Thanks again, Dr. Malaika. I'll see you in two weeks," Raquel said.

26

"Ladies, here we are. I pray our beautiful home is always full of love and laughter," Jermaine said as he pulled into the driveway of their beautiful home. "Before we go in, there is something I would like to do. Shela, may I have your hand?"

"Yes, Honey." Shela reached out her hand.

"Shela, my wife, thank you for loving me despite all my faults and mishaps. I appreciate you from the bottom of my heart. I promise to be all the man you deserve, and more, and to love you and my son for the rest of our lives." At that moment, he pulled out a little pretty blue box. "Here is a fourteen-karat white gold necklace for you, Baby, with a blue diamond to represent our handsome son."

"Jermaine," Shela said with tears in her eyes. "Baby, you are everything to me, and I trust you with everything in me. I love you, Jermaine, for the rest of our lives. Thank you so much, Baby. This means so much to me."

"Shela, you are welcome."

Jermaine reached back to touch Raquel's left shoulder with his right hand. "Raquel, my baby girl, my firstborn, because of you I have kept my sanity. Raising you was my whole reason for living. We lost a lot through the years, but in the last year, we gained more than we could ever ask for. I promise to be the daddy you deserve and to love you and my daughter for the rest of our lives."

Jermaine then pulled out a little pretty pink box. "Here is a fourteen-karat white gold necklace for you, with a pink diamond to represent our beautiful baby girl."

"Daddy, you have been my everything all my life," Raquel said, putting her left hand on top of her dad's. "You are why I am who I am, and I know you are a promise keeper. Thanks for finding Shela and bringing her into our lives. Daddy, I love you and I always will."

Hell no! I must be crazy! Am I delusional? Lord, help me, please! Unexpectedly, Shela had a flashback of the night her world fell apart and all she heard was Raquel's voice playing over and over in her head screaming, *'Dad, you did this to me,'* as soon as Jermaine touched Raquel's shoulder and handed over the necklace. She was able to keep her composure, but the disgusting thought of Jermaine and his daughter was killing her inside. *Oh my God! What am I doing? What was I thinking? This man is selfish, did he just give his daughter and grandchild or daughter the same necklace he gave to me, his wife, and our son? This love ain't blind or stupid—or is it! I feel like I just woke up! I thought I was fine, but Lord I can't do this!*

They all walked into their home as Jermaine proudly carried Jermaine IV and Shermaine.

My Daddy's Baby Too
The Aftermath

Coming Soon!!!!!

Tyler Perry,

I would love for you to read my book and I hope one day we can work together and do a movie. Please Enjoy

Charmaine Marie

Thank you in advance!